EXPLORING CHINA

A CHILDREN'S GUIDE TO CHINESE CULTURE

Editor-in-chief: Fu Siyi

Compilers: Hu Ailin Yang Fanzhi Peng Li Yan Weilin

Senior English Editor: Nia Jones

First Edition 2015

ISBN 978-7-5138-0639-8

Published by Sinolingua Co., Ltd
24 Baiwanzhuang Road, Beijing 100037, China
Tel: (86)10-68320585, 68997826
Fax: (86)10-68997826, 68326333
http://www.sinolingua.com.cn
E-mail: hyjx@sinolingua.com.cn
Facebook: www.facebook.com/sinolingua
Printed by Beijing Chengshunda Printing Co., Ltd

Printed in the People's Republic of China

Introduction

Welcome to *Exploring China — A children's guide to Chinese culture*!

What is this resource pack?

This is a multi-media teaching resource pack intended for primary school children to learn about Chinese culture, although with some adaptation the material can be used for secondary school students.

This resource pack contains:

- A fully illustrated textbook
- Two discs containing video clips, animated stories and computer games
- A comprehensive Teacher's Guide
- Eight Fact Sheets, each highlighting the key learning points in the unit

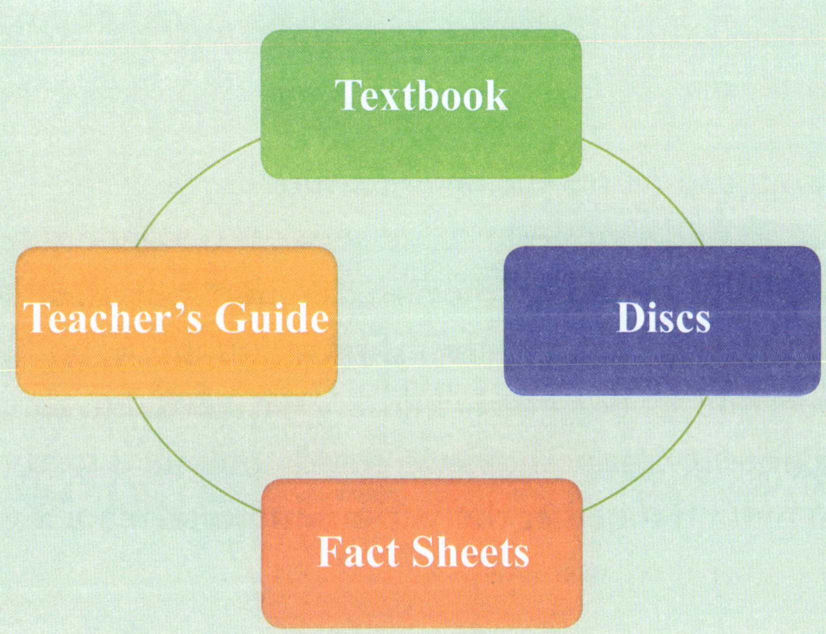

Why was this resource pack developed?

This pack was developed while we were teaching Chinese in schools in Wales, the United Kingdom. We found that our pupils were fascinated in learning about China through the cultural workshops we organised for them, and their fascination for Chinese culture usually motivated their interest in learning the language. We started to think: Could we teach Chinese culture, in a didactic sense, to our pupils so that they would develop a more structured knowledge of China?

This initial question has led to many further questions: How could we teach culture, as compared with language? How could we teach Chinese culture to young learners whose cognitive style is distinctively different from adults? How could we make "Chinese things" comprehensible to our pupils who have been brought up in Western cultures? How could we present historical facts and cultural knowledge, which may be profound in nature, in an easy and engaging manner so that our young pupils can understand and enjoy learning about China? Where could we source teaching materials? …

In our search for some off-the-shelf textbooks, we were disappointed to find that none could serve as a standard textbook for teaching Chinese culture to overseas school pupils, although there were many for teaching the Chinese language, both for adult learners and school-aged children. We started to think, rather ambitiously, that perhaps we could compile a textbook on our own by putting together the various materials that we had used in our cultural workshops.

Fulfilling that ambition turned out to be a challenging and lengthy journey. To begin with, we were beset with further concerns: How could we select the material from the rich treasure house of Chinese culture, and what should be the criteria for selection? How could we maintain the academic quality of a textbook, but at the same time incorporate fun and motivating elements? How could we reconcile depth of knowledge with simplicity in our approach? How could we remain objective and historical without giving an impression of making political propaganda?...

It took more than a year for us to resolve our questions, though not to our complete satisfaction. We produced draft after draft of the Student's Book and revised again and again the story and video scripts. Meanwhile, we had regular meetings with our local education specialist, Mrs. Nia Jones, the Language Teaching Adviser at CILT Cymru (The National Centre for Languages in Wales). Our initial intention of writing a textbook eventually became a rather comprehensive project which developed into a multi-media teaching resource pack, to be used not only for our own pupils in Wales, but also for school pupils worldwide!

This teaching resource pack is therefore a product of teamwork led by Professor Fu Siyi while she was working as the Academic Director at the Confucius Institute of Cardiff University. It represents the joint efforts of our four local tutors and the contributions from language and education specialists, both from China and the UK.

How to use this resource pack?

To facilitate easy management of the pack, here is further information about each component of it.

I. The Textbook for Students

There are eight units in the textbook, each covering a particular aspect of Chinese culture. The contents of the eight units are:

1. LAND (China's geographical location, land features, mountains & rivers, climate, animals & plants, and administrative divisions)

2. PEOPLE (China's population, ethnic groups, Chinese families & homes, and daily life of Chinese people)

3. HISTORY (China's best-known historical figures and events)

4. LANGUAGE (the earliest Chinese written records, Mandarin Chinese and local dialects, Chinese characters & pinyin, and calligraphy)

5. EDUCATION (Confucius, ancient Chinese schools, the Imperial Examination, and education in China today)

6. SCIENCE AND TECHNOLOGY (the Four Great Inventions, Chinese Blue-and-white Porcelain, pioneers of traditional Chinese medicine, the early Chinese seismograph, the invention of hybrid rice, and space walks by Chinese astronauts)

7. FESTIVALS (the Chinese lunar calendar, Spring Festival, Lantern Festival, Tomb Sweeping Festival, Dragon Boat Festival, Mid-autumn Festival, and National Day)

8. TOURISM (the Great Wall, the Forbidden City, the Terracotta Warriors and the Huangshan Mountain)

The pupils are guided through four learning stages in each unit:

1. First, they are challenged with QUESTIONS, which indicate the learning outcomes or the learning areas in the unit.

2. Then, they watch a VIDEO, which highlights the key learning points covered in the unit.

3. Following the video, the pupils read the TEXT, which is broken down into sections, each focusing on a particular learning point.

4. After reading the text, the pupils take part in a variety of ACTIVITIES, ranging from stories, hands-on activities, games and mini-projects.

The sequence of these four learning stages is reflected through the headings used in the textbook, illustrated as below:

- **Let's find out** - projecting learning areas
- **Let's watch a video** - highlighting key messages
- **Let's find out more** - presenting knowledge & facts
- **Activity time** - reinforcing what has been learnt

II. The Discs

In order to make the learning process fun and engaging, each unit is supplemented with a video, one or two animated stories and some interactive games, all carefully chosen to relate to the theme and content of the unit. These are provided in two discs, which contains eight video clips, 12 animated stories and 20 games. Directions and guidance for using these resources are provided in the Teacher's Guide.

Activities and games in the discs are designed in order to enhance pupils' learning or to check their understanding, although they appear as entertainment. This is indeed a feature that distinguishes this teaching resource pack from traditional teaching materials.

III. The Teacher's Guide

The Teacher's Guide is organised to this format in each unit:

1. Teaching objectives & summary of contents
2. About the video
3. Notes on each section
4. Guide to activities and games
5. Script of stories

Each of the five parts contains detailed information and guidance for the teacher. This aims to save the time that the teacher would normally spend on preparation. We also hope that the detailed guidance provided for the teacher will make it possible for someone who is not necessarily a specialist in Chinese culture to lead a Chinese culture class.

IV. The Fact Sheets

There is a Fact Sheet for each unit, designed as individual loose sheets for children to use for revision. These will be especially useful when the pupils do not have their own copies of the textbook. The Fact Sheet is printed on both sides: the front lists the key points that the pupils are expected to have learnt from the unit, while the back provides some knowledge or information that is not covered in the textbook, but related to what pupils have learnt in that particular unit. We hope that this will further engage the pupils and expand their learning.

What is special about this resource pack?

Parts of this teaching resource pack have been used by our tutors at schools in Wales and have been very well received. The teaching resources we have provided in the pack have been found to be:

- Informative — covering a wide range of topics and providing facts and knowledge in simple language, suitable for school pupils
- Interactive — engaging pupils in various activities rather than merely citing knowledge

- Interesting — making learning fun and engaging with a fresh teaching approach
- Flexible — easy to use in parts as supplements to such general school modules as History, Social Studies, Sciences etc., though the pack itself provides ideal teaching materials for an individual Chinese module

How to contact us?

We hope that you will find this multi-media teaching resource pack useful, and that both you and your pupils will enjoy using it. We value your feedback, so please let us know if you have any comments or suggestions.

Editor-in-chief: Prof Fu Siyi

E-mail: syfu@xmu.edu.cn

Contents

Unit 1 Land 2

Unit 2 People 22

Unit 3 History 44

Unit 4 Language 68

Unit 5 Education 94

Unit 6 Science and Technology 120

Unit 7 Festivals 144

Unit 8 Tourism 172

Land

UNIT 1

1. China's Geographic Location
2. China's Land Features
3. Mountains, Deserts and Rivers
4. Climate
5. Animals and Plants
6. Regions, Provinces and Cities

Let's find out

- Where is China and how big is it?
- Does China have any special land features?
- What are China's famous mountains and rivers?
- What is the climate like in China?
- What animals and plants are unique to China?
- What are the regions, provinces and cities of China?

Let's watch a video

1. China's Geographic Location

- Where is China located in the map of the world?
- What are China's neighbouring countries?

China is in East Asia on the western shore of the Pacific Ocean. It has an area of about 9,600,000 square kilometres, the third largest in the world.

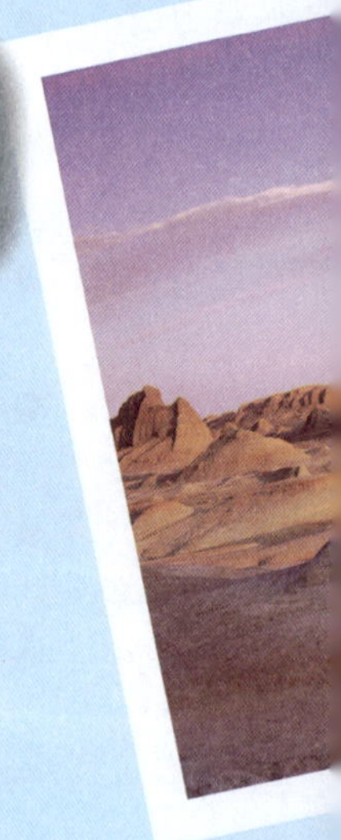

MAP OF THE WORLD

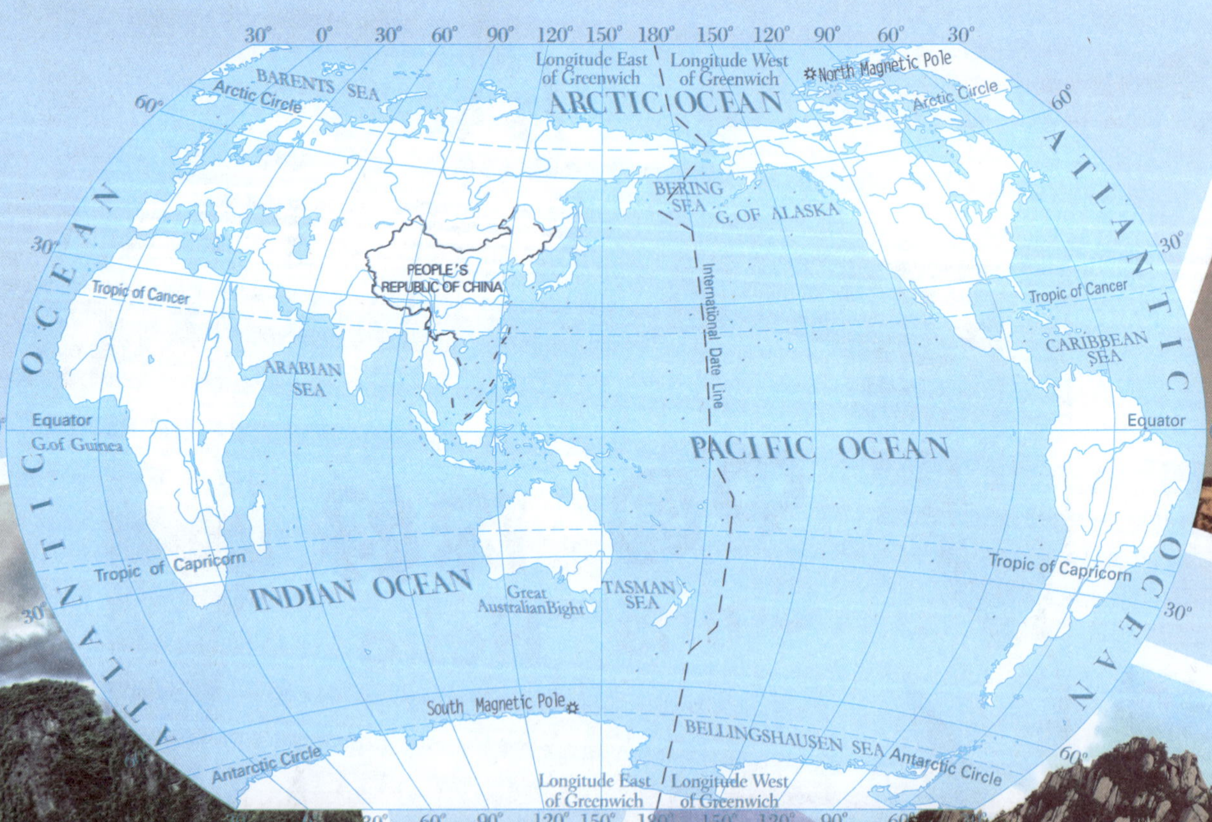

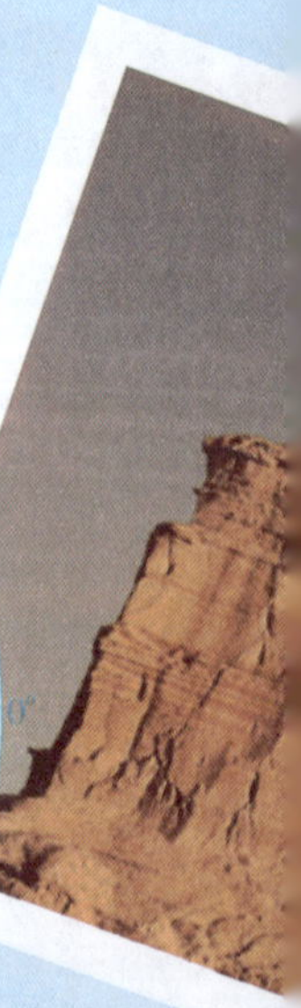

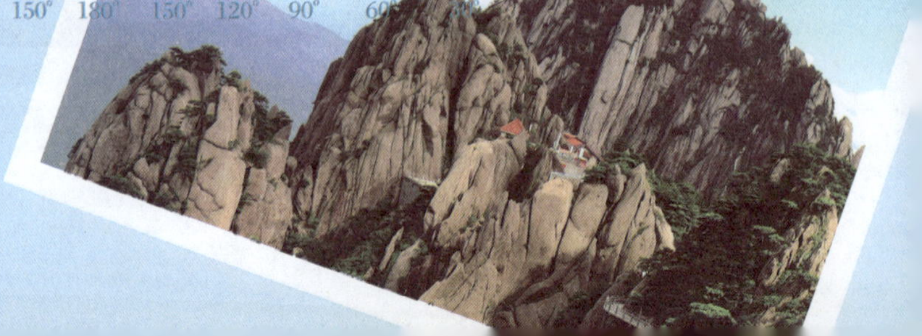

PEOPLE'S REPUBLIC OF CHINA
ARCTIC OCEAN
PACIFIC OCEAN
INDIAN OCEAN
ATLANTIC OCEAN
BARENTS SEA
BERING SEA
G. OF ALASKA
ARABIAN SEA
CARIBBEAN SEA
TASMAN SEA
BELLINGSHAUSEN SEA
Great Australian Bight
G.of Guinea
North Magnetic Pole
South Magnetic Pole
Arctic Circle
Tropic of Cancer
Equator
Tropic of Capricorn
Antarctic Circle
International Date Line
Longitude East of Greenwich
Longitude West of Greenwich

BORDERS

China borders with 14 countries along a boundary of more than 20,000 kilometres, with the Democratic Republic of Korea to the east; Russia, Mongolia, Kazakhstan, Kyrgyzstan and Tajikistan to the north, northeast and northwest; Afghanistan, Pakistan, India, Nepal and Bhutan to the west and southwest; and Vietnam, Laos and Myanmar to the south.

China's coastline stretches 14,500 kilometres. It is surrounded by the Pacific Ocean to the east and there are more than 5000 islands lying off the coast.

Activity time

1. JOIN the dots to reveal the image. What shape does it look like?

2. LOOK at the map of the world and find China. Use a coloured pen to OUTLINE the country. And then ANSWER the following questions.

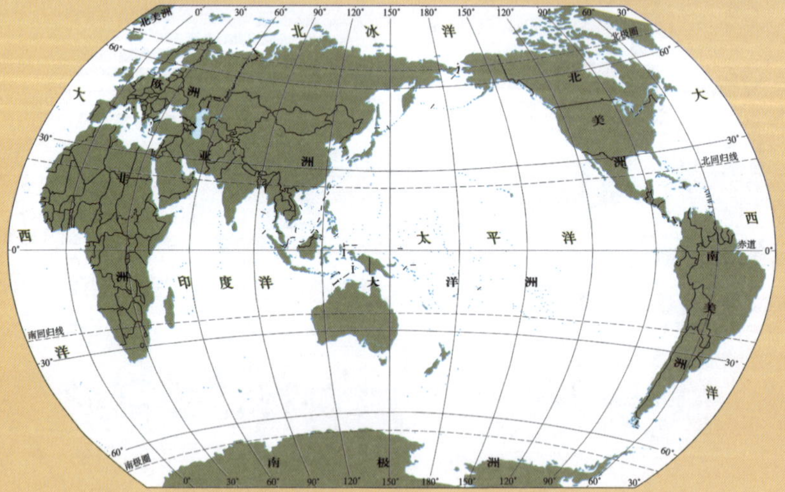

1) Do you know how big your country is?
My country has an area of ________ km^2.
It is _______ (bigger/smaller) than China.

2) Do you know which are the two largest countries in the world?
No. 1 __________ No. 2 ___________

2. China's Land Features

- Is China flat or mountainous?
- How much of China's land is used for farming?

China's landscapes in different colours

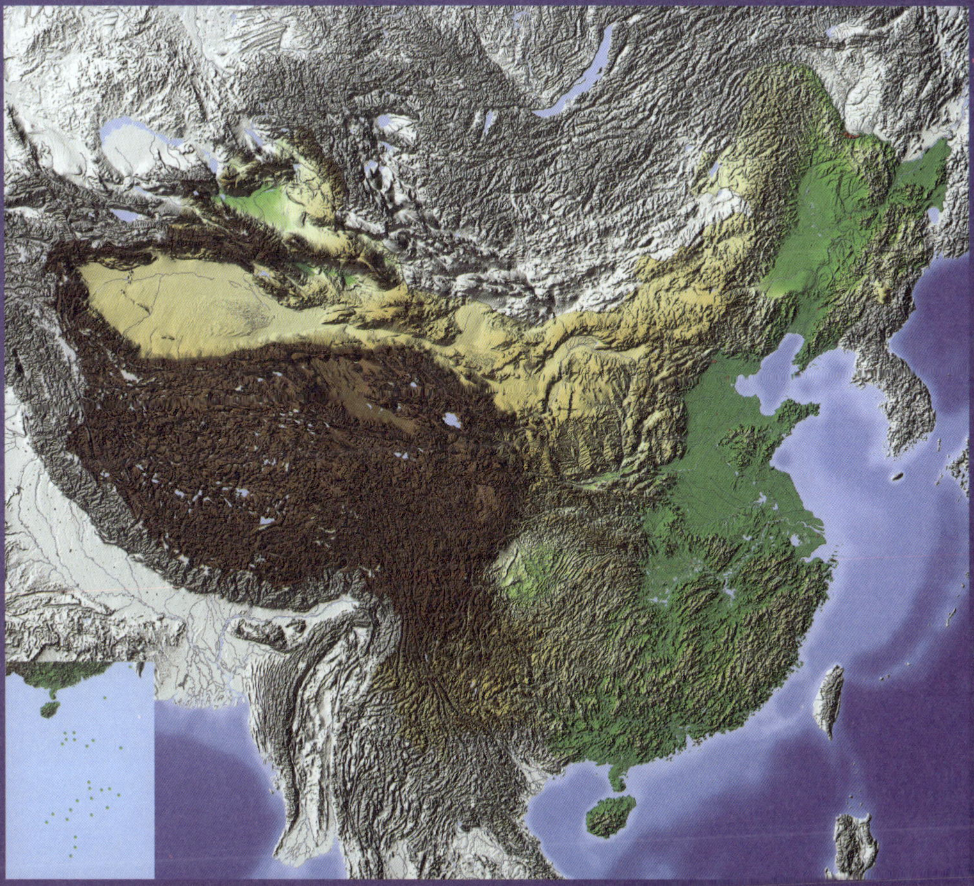

- flat land
- highlands and basins
- mountainous areas

Land

You can see from the map that there are a lot of mountains in the west and the country becomes more and more flat as you move east. If you have a bird's-eye view of China you will find that the land lowers gradually from west to east like a staircase in three tiers.

In the southwest (in brown) is the Qinghai-Tibet Plateau, known as "the Roof of the World". The Plateau is 4000 metres above sea level and is known as the 1st tier. This is where Mount Everest, the world's highest peak is located.

To the north and east of the Qinghai-Tibet Plateau lie the highlands and basins (in yellow). This area is 1100 to 2000 metres above sea level and is known as the 2nd tier.

In the east (in green) are rolling hills and flat lands. This area is no more than 500 metres above sea level and is known as the 3rd tier.

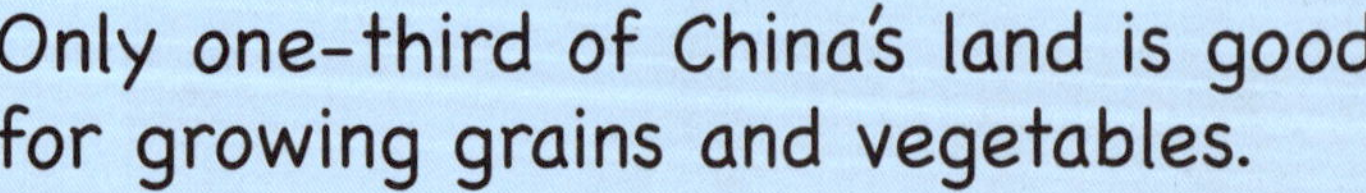

Only one-third of China's land is good for growing grains and vegetables.

THREE TIERS: In which tier do these people live? Note the numbers on the boards.

Tier 1	Tier 2	Tier 3

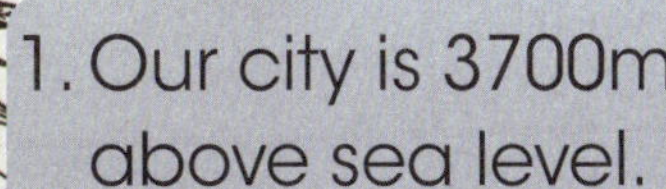

1. Our city is 3700m above sea level.

2. Our city is 1200m above sea level.

3. Our city is 500m above sea level.

4. My city is where the world's highest peak is located.

5. My city is a very rich city near the East China Sea.

6. My city is the capital of China.

3. Mountains, Deserts and Rivers

- What are China's most famous mountains, deserts and rivers?
- What is special about them?

Two thirds of China's land is mountainous. **Mount Everest**, the highest peak in the world, is located in the Qinghai-Tibet Plateau, amid the Himalaya Range on the border between Nepal and China. The word Himalayas means "home of the snow", because the Himalaya Mountains are high enough to always have snow on them. No plants grow near the peak due to powerful winds, extremely low temperatures, and a lack of oxygen.

There are also dry deserts in China. The two most famous deserts are the **Gobi Desert** and the **Taklamakan Desert.**

The Gobi Desert is the fifth largest in The world and the largest in Asia. It covers parts of northern and northwestern China, and southern Mongolia. The Gobi is famous in history for being part of the great Mongol Empire.

The Taklamakan Desert is one of the largest sandy deserts in the world. It is nicknamed the Sea of Death because of its poisonous snakes and frequent sand storms.

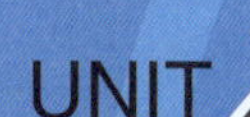

China is well-known for two mighty rivers: **the Yangtze River** and **the Yellow River**.

The Yangtze River is the longest river in China and the third longest in the world. It flows for 6418 km from the Qinghai-Tibet Plateau eastwards all the way to Shanghai before emptying into the East China Sea. The Yangtze River basin is home to one-third of China's population.

The Yellow River used to be nicknamed China's Sorrow because it flooded every year and destroyed many homes in the area. Since ancient times, people have had to build barriers to protect themselves against flooding. In modern times, the river has been stable since large dams were built and forests were planted. The tree roots take up water and hold the soil and stop it from being washed away.

1. Surviving the flood: If there is a flood, life buoys and life jackets may save your life. Can you think of other things that could also be helpful? Draw pictures of them and explain why they would be helpful.

Do you know?
The Three Gorges is a scenic area along the Yangtze River with a length of about 200km.

E-game

Can you dodge the snow balls and reach the peak?

- What is the weather like in China?

China is a vast country and has different climates. From north to south, China can be divided into six climate zones:

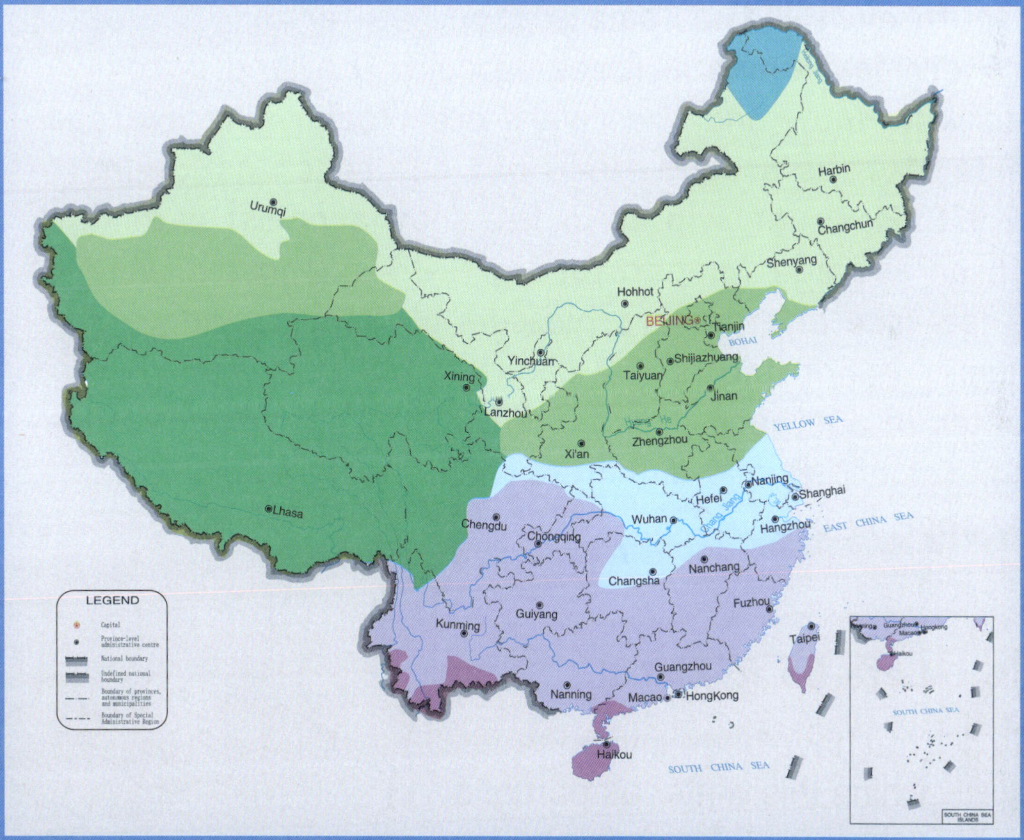

The Six Climate Zones

	Winter	Summer
Cold-temperate Zone	-31°C~-15°C	18°C~23°C
Mild-temperate Zone	below 0°C	10°C~20°C
Warm-temperate Zone	below 0°C	above 20°C
Subtropical Zone	above 0°C	above 28°C
Tropical Zone	above 18°C	28°C~40°C
Plateau Climate Zone	-16°C~0°C	above 22°C

The temperature varies greatly from north to south even in the same season. Winter in northernmost China is freezing cold. The land is covered with snow and the rivers are frozen. The average temperature is around -10°C but can reach as low as -52.3°C. However, winter in the southernmost is mild, with an average temperature of 22.9°C. Most areas are ice-free and flowers blossom all year round. Summer is hot across the country, but it is much shorter in northern areas. Southern areas usually have long, hot and humid summers, and the temperature may soar to over 40°C.

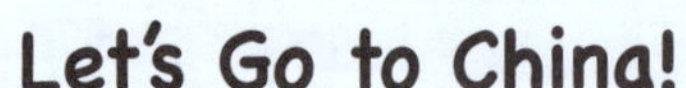

E-game

Let's Go to China!

You have been invited to China this winter as part of a school visit. There will be two groups. Group A will be visiting Haikou and Group B Beijing. Choose what you think each group should take with them from the list of the objects provided. Drag and drop the items into the luggage bag of each group and give your reasons for choosing them.

5. Animals and Plants

- What animals and plants are unique to China?

China's wildlife is very diverse. There are more than 100 animal species unique to China, including the giant panda, the golden monkey, the white-lipped deer, the Yangtze River dolphin, the Chinese alligator, the south China tiger and the red-crowned crane.

China also has the most abundant plant life in the world, and has more than 32,000 species of plants. It is home to more than 2000 species of edible plants and over 3000 species of medicinal plants.

Some plants can only be found in China, such as the dawn redwood and the golden larch.

The dawn redwood, a very tall tree, is considered to be one of the oldest and rarest plants in the world.

The golden larch, one of the rarest types of trees in the world, grows in the Yangtze River valley. Its coin-shaped leaves on short branches are green in spring and summer, and turn yellow in autumn.

There are many beautiful flowers in China. The peony is treasured as one of China's national flowers. It is also known as "The Queen of Flowers" as it has large blossoms, many petals and bright colours.

Let's listen to a story

The story of the peony

Follow-up activities

1. Who was Wu Zetian? What happened between her and the peony?
2. Draw pictures to represent the story.
3. Retell the story in your own words.

1. MATCH the words with the images.

dawn redwood

peony

golden larch

2. FOLLOW the steps below and DRAW your own giant panda.

3. COLOUR the peonies.

6. Regions, Provinces and Cities

- What is the capital of China?
- How many regions are there in China?

Look at this map, which shows the regions, provinces and cities of China in different colours.

XINJIANG UYGUR AUTONOMOUS REGION
Urumqi
XIZANG AUTONOMOUS REGION
Lhasa
Qomolangma Feng
QINGHAI
Xining
GANSU
Lanzhou
NINGXIA
Yinchuan
NEI MONGOL AUTONOMOUS REGION
Hohhot
HEILONGJIANG
Harbin
JILIN
Changchun
LIAONING
Shenyang
BEIJING
BEIJINGSHI
TIANJINSHI
Tianjin
HEBEI
Shijiazhuang
BOHAI
SHANXI
Taiyuan
SHANDONG
Jinan
YELLOW SEA
SHAANXI
Xi'an
HENAN
Zhengzhou
JIANGSU
Nanjing
ANHUI
Hefei
SHANGHAISHI
Shanghai
SICHUAN
Chengdu
CHONGQINGSHI
Chongqing
HUBEI
Wuhan
ZHEJIANG
Hangzhou
EAST CHINA SEA
GUIZHOU
Guiyang
HUNAN
Changsha
JIANGXI
Nanchang
FUJIAN
Fuzhou
Taipei
TAIWAN
YUNNAN
Kunming
GUANGXI ZHUANG AUTONOMOUS REGION
Nanning
GUANGZHOU
Guangzhou
Macao
MACAO S.A.R.
HongKong
HONGKONG S.A.R.
HAINAN
Haikou
SOUTH CHINA SEA

LEGEND
Municipalities
Provinces
Autonomous Regions
Special Administrative Regions

If you look closely, you will find that there are 23 provinces, five autonomous regions, four municipalities and two special administrative regions. The capital city of China is Beijing.

The autonomous regions are mainly inhabited by non-Han ethnic groups, they are:

The four municipalities are the major cities: Beijing, Tianjin, Shanghai and Chongqing.

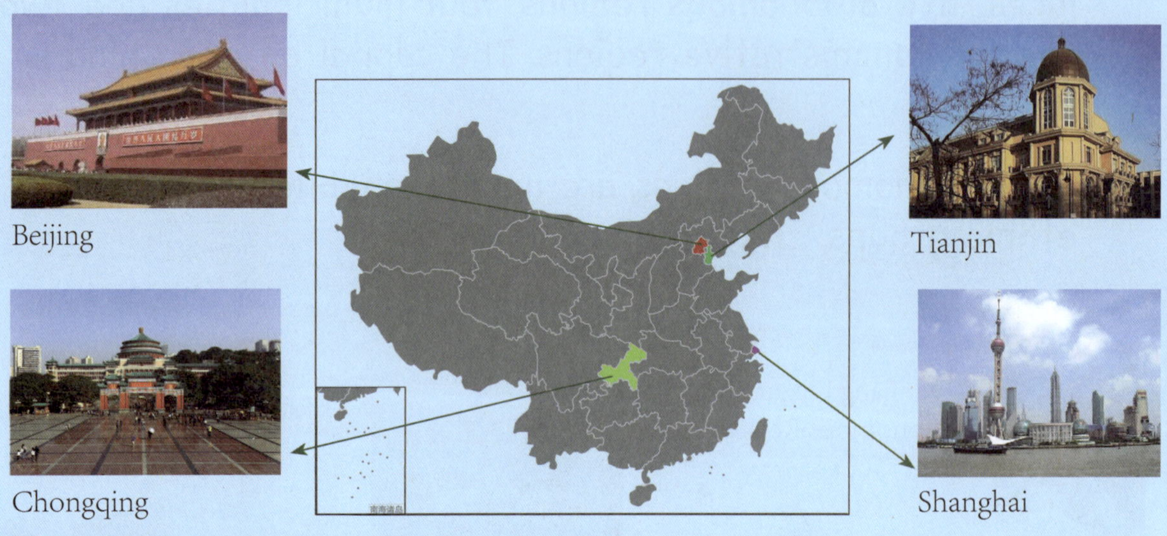

The two special administrative regions are Hong Kong and Macao.

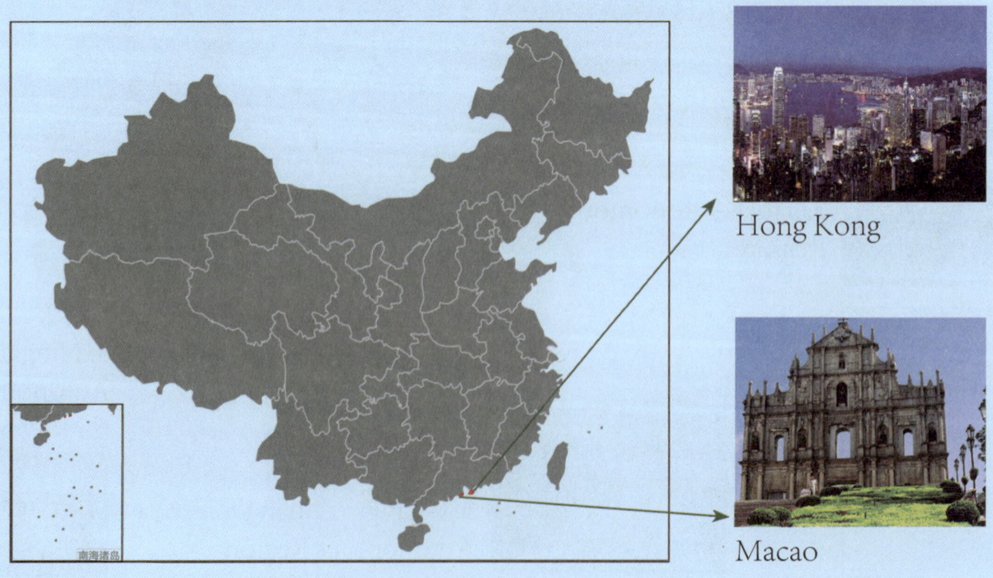

Activity time

Map of China Jigsaw Puzzle

You will be shown some regional maps of the provinces, municipalities, autonomous regions and special administrative regions of China in each round. Drag and drop as quickly as you can each regional map into their proper location on the map of China.

People

UNIT 2

1. China's Population
2. The Han People and Other Ethnic Groups
3. Chinese Families
4. Chinese Weddings and Marriages
5. Chinese Homes
6. Celebrating Birthdays in China

Let's find out

- How many people live in China?
- How many ethnic groups are there in China?
- What is life like in a Chinese family?
- What do Chinese homes look like?
- How do people celebrate their birthdays?

Let's watch a video

- **How many people live in China now?**
- **Which part of China has the largest population?**
- **Which part of China has the smallest population?**

China has a population of over 1.3 billion people, the largest in the world. One in every five people on the planet lives in China. More people live in the eastern coastal areas, while fewer people live in the western mountainous areas. For example, many people live in the east in cities such as Shanghai, where population density reaches about 400 people per square kilometre. In areas in the west like Tibet, the population density is as low as two people per square kilometre.

The number of people who live in cities and rural areas also differs slightly: 53.73% of the total population of China live in cities while 46.27% live in rural areas.

Rural
Population
46.27%

1. COLOUR this map of China to show the different number of people who live in the different areas, and then ANSWER the following question.

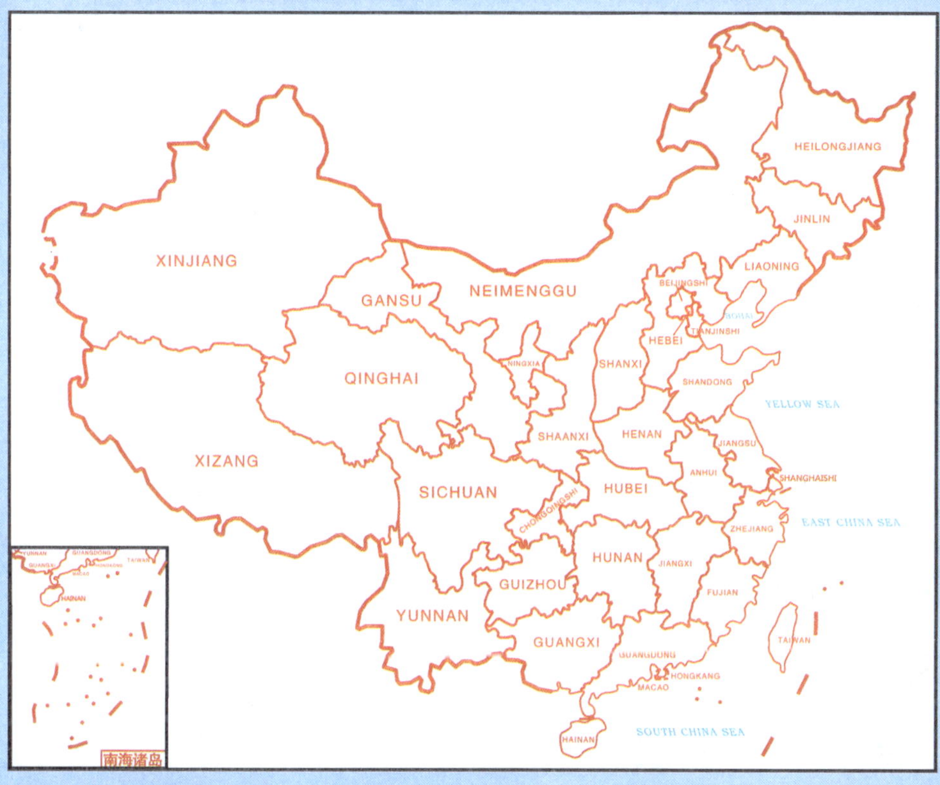

- where the largest number of people live
- where many other people live
- where the least number of people live

Question: Why do more people live in the east than in the west of China? Use some of the following hints to help you answer this question.

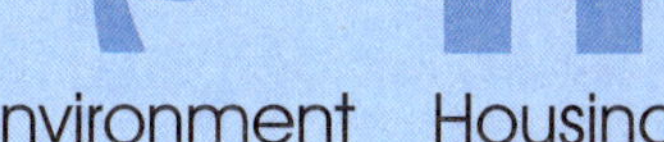
Environment

Housing

Transport

Weather

2. The Han People and Other Ethnic Groups

- How many ethnic groups are there in China?
- What is special about them?

There are 56 ethnic groups in China, including the Han people, which make up over 90% of the total population.

Each ethnic group has its own culture and traditions. Some ethnic groups speak their own languages. They dress in their own national costumes too.

The Tibetans live in very high mountainous areas in southwestern China, where Mount Everest, the world's highest peak is located. The Tibetans have a special tradition of presenting Hada, a long piece of silk, to their dear friends or beloved ones as a token of respect and affection.

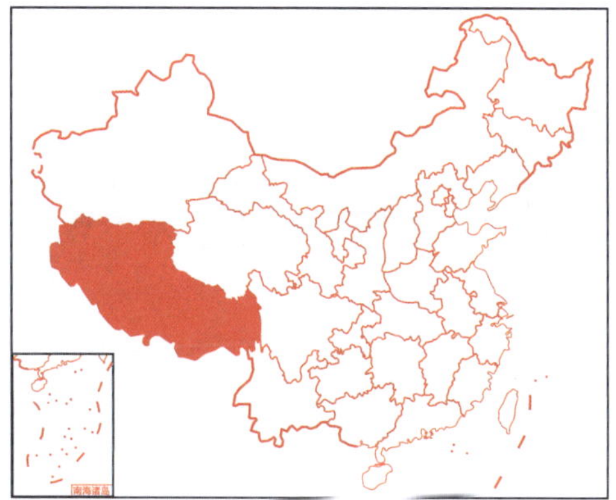

The Uygur live in northwest China. They live in "the Land of Fruits", known worldwide for its production of seedless grapes and sweet melons.

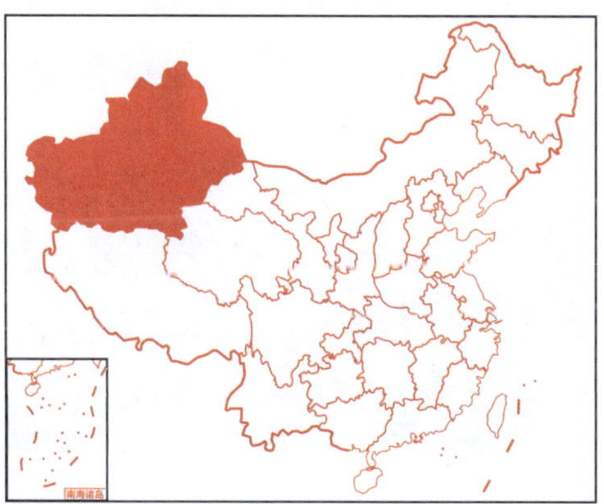

The Mongolians live in north China. They are known for travelling on horses and camels. They eat a lot of meat and drink salty tea. They are very good at hunting, horse racing and wrestling.

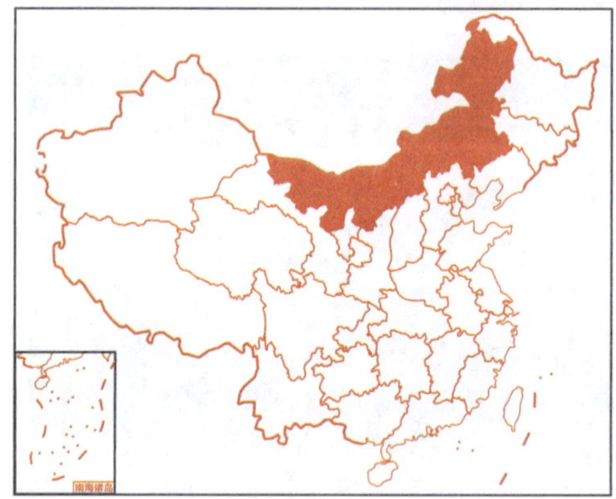

Living in midland China, towards the north, are **the Hui** people. They practise Islam, and many of them are direct descendants of Silk Road travellers.

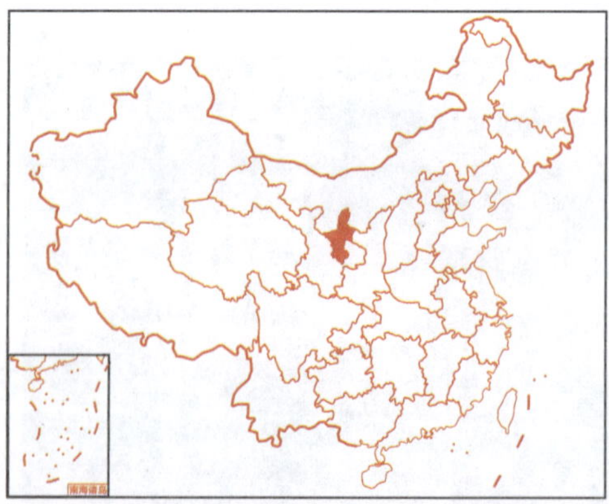

The Manchu people live in the northeast. They conquered the central plain of China in 1644 and ruled the country for over 200 years until 1911, when the Qing Dynasty collapsed.

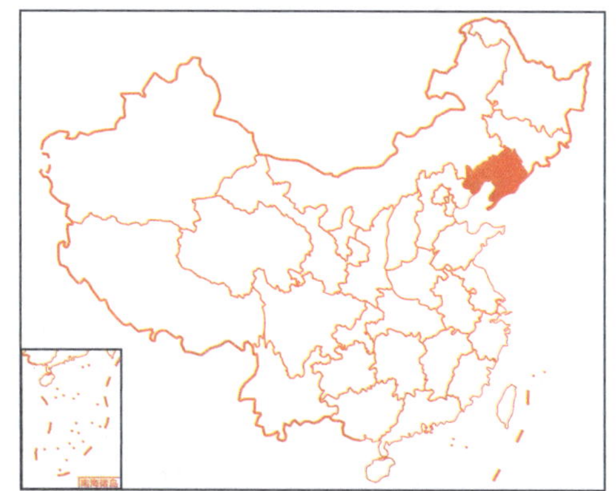

Other important ethnic groups include:

The Zhuang

The Yi

The Miao

The Bouyei

The Koreans

The Tujia

The Yao

Most ethnic groups are very musical, and are well-known for their songs and dances.

The Bai

The Naxi

The Dai

1. Finding out their hometowns

Here are the pictures of some ethnic groups in China. Drag and drop the images to where you think they live on the map.

2. Dressing up

Dress the girls in different ethnic costumes.

Let's listen to a story

The story of Ashima

Follow-up activities

1. Answer the following questions:
   - Who is Ahei?
   - Who won the singing contest?
   - What happened between Ashima and Ahei on their way home?

2. Retell the story in your own words.

3. Colour the portrait of Ashima by using your imagination.

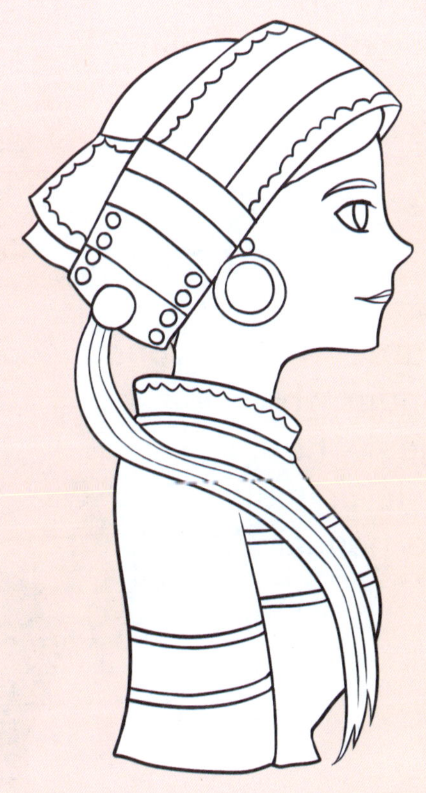

3. Chinese Families

- How have Chinese families changed?
- When do Chinese people get married and what do they do on their wedding day?

This is the word "family" written in Chinese:
It is a pictographic character. The upper part of it 宀 looks like the roof of a house, and the lower part of it 豕 is a pictographic character for "pig", which has developed from a picture like this:

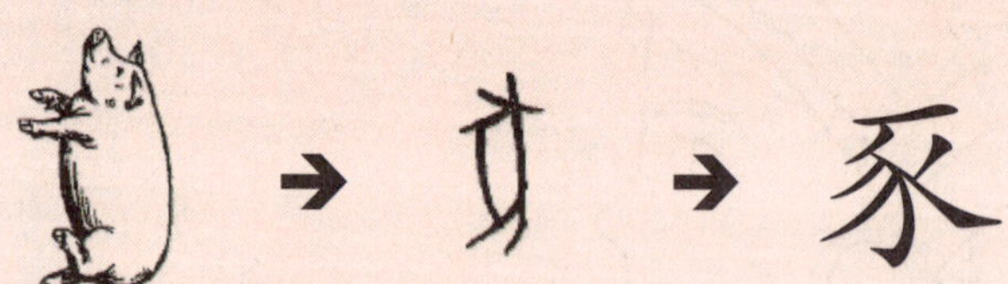

The image of the character 家 (pronounced as "jiā") with a pig under the roof of a house may suggest the importance of domestic animals to traditional Chinese households.

Chinese families used to be very big and it was common for four generations to live under the same roof.

Since the 1970s, Chinese families have been getting smaller and smaller. It is now common for couples to have only one child.

A traditional family

A nuclear family

In the past:

- The head of the family, usually the oldest male in the household, had complete power over all family business.
- Only the male could carry on the family line. So, the first born boy was the dearest child in the household.
- Only boys went to school. Girls stayed at home to help with the housework.

- Women's role was taking care of household duties and domestic chores.

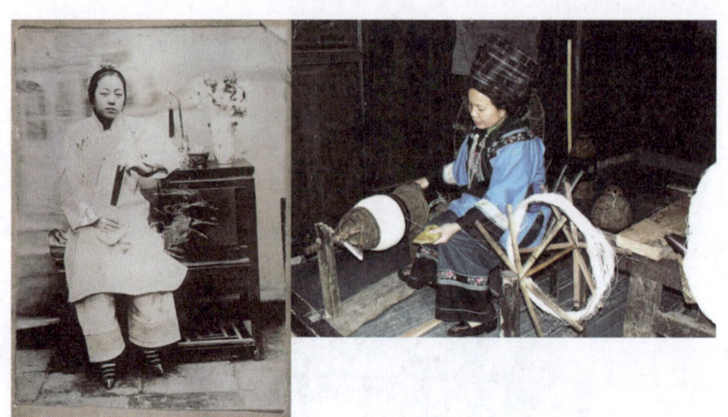

In present day China:

- Men and women are considered equal in the family and they share housework.
- Both boys and girls go to school.
- Women go to work and are treated and paid the same as men.

COMPARE the Chinese family with your own family. What do you have in common and what are the differences? WRITE your notes in the space provided.

Chinese Family

My family

Things in Common	Differences
________________	________________
________________	________________
________________	________________
________________	________________

4. Chinese Weddings and Marriages

- How are couples dressed on their wedding day?
- How do people celebrate their wedding?
- What kinds of gifts do the couples receive?
- What changes have taken place in Chinese weddings and marriages?

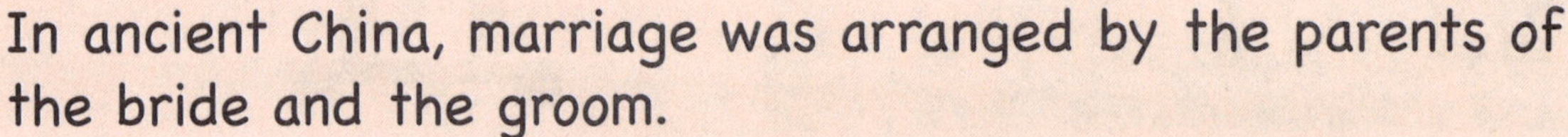

In ancient China, marriage was arranged by the parents of the bride and the groom.

Nowadays, people can choose who they want to marry.

According to the law in China, men can get married at the age of 22 and women at 20. For all Chinese people, marriage is one of the most important things in their lives.

An arranged marriage

A love marriage

As Chinese people have become better off, they have started to spend more money on their weddings. Great changes have taken place in the way they plan and organise their weddings.

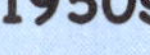

	1950s	1970s	since the 1990s
How the couple are dressed			
How the wedding is celebrated			
What gifts the couple receive			

Do you know?

1. Chinese women still keep their surnames after they get married.
2. Chinese people believe that red is a lucky colour, so many brides wear red gowns on their wedding day.

Activity time

1. Chinese paper cutting: “Double Happiness”

2. CHOOSE a wedding gift for a Chinese couple. EXPLAIN why you choose your gift.

A. A bunch of flowers.

B. A wedding cake.

C. A box of chocolates.

D. A red envelope with money inside.

5. Chinese Homes

- What kind of houses do Chinese people live in?
- What do their homes look like?

People in China live in different types of houses. In northern China, typically in Beijing, people used to live in **Siheyuan**, meaning "four-sided enclosed courtyard".

In areas south of the Yangtze River, people live in houses with white walls and black tiled roofs, known as **Jiangnan houses**.

The Uygurs in the Xinjiang Uygur Autonomous Region live in a variation of **stilt houses**.

Many ethnic groups in the southwestern provinces live in **Diaojiaolou**.

The Mongolians live in **yurts**, which are oddly shaped, but very comfortable.

The Hakka people in southeast China live in *Tulou*, or "Earth Buildings".

In some areas of northwest China, people live in houses carved like caves, known as **Yaodong**.

The Dai people, in the rainforest areas in southwest China, live in **bamboo houses**.

The insides of these homes are also different. For example, Yaodongs are usually six metres deep and four metres wide. Like caves, they are warm in winter and cool in summer and receive little natural light. By contrast, the bamboo houses are built with bamboo only. Their beams, pillars and walls are all made of bamboo. A bamboo house usually has two or three bedrooms and a sitting room with a brazier used for cooking.

However, Chinese people today are getting used to living in apartments. In cities and towns, some people also live in large houses.

A modern Chinese home usually includes a living room, two or three bedrooms, a bathroom and a kitchen.

Activity time

DRAW a picture of the type of house in China you would like to live in. Where would you like it to be? MAKE a list of the rooms and the things that you would like your house to have in it and EXPLAIN why you choose each of them.

6. Celebrating Birthdays in China

- How do people celebrate a baby's first birthday?
- How do young and elderly people celebrate their birthdays?

Birthdays are very important to the Chinese. When a baby turns one year old, it is common for the family to invite close friends and relatives to celebrate the baby's birthday. In some areas of China, the first birthday is celebrated with special rituals. For instance, one tradition is to make predictions about the baby's future career and fortune. They place the baby in the centre of a group of objects, and let him or her "choose" any of the objects. The object they pick will give a clue as to what the baby will be in the future. This is known as "zhuazhou".

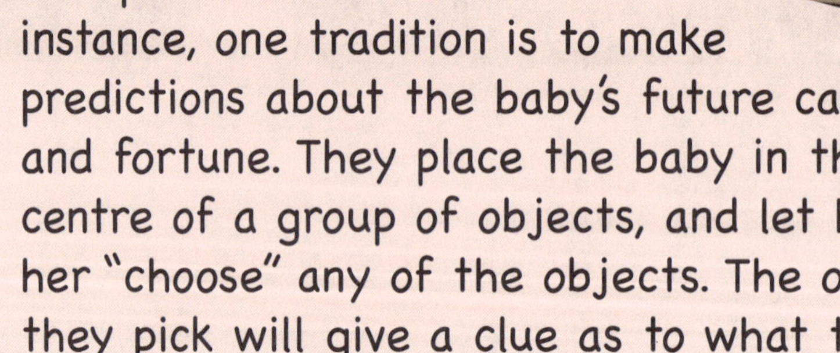

Young people celebrate their birthdays by having a birthday cake with candles and inviting their friends or relatives to share a meal with them.

Older people have special celebrations for their 50th and 60th birthdays. Together with their family members, they eat "long-life noodles" on their birthdays. The longer the noodles, the better, as this symbolises their long life.

1. MAKE a birthday gift for an older family member.

Step 1: Colour the Chinese character "shou" (shown below, which means "long life") in red.

Step 2: Place it on the paper provided and start decorating it as you wish.

Step 3: Take it home and give it to your older family member.

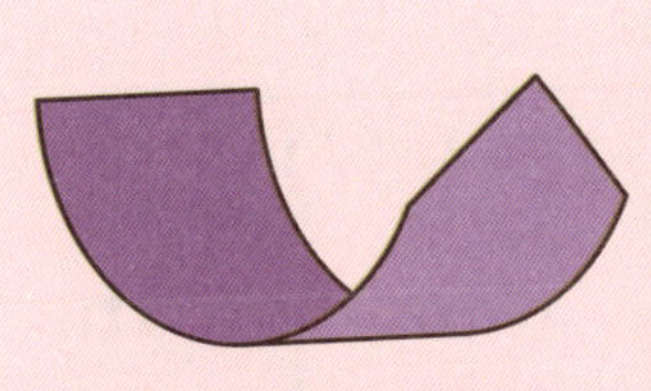

2. Let's SING the "Happy Birthday" song in Chinese.

Happy birthday to you,

Happy birthday to you,

Happy birthday to ____ (child's name),

Happy birthday to you.

Zhù nǐ shēngrì kuàilè,
祝 你 生日 快乐，
zhù nǐ shēngrì kuàilè,
祝 你 生日 快乐，
zhù _____ shēngrì kuàilè,
祝 _____ 生日 快乐，
zhù nǐ shēngrì kuàilè.
祝 你 生日 快乐。

History

UNIT 3

1. The Ancestors of the Chinese People (before 2070 BC)
2. Qin Shi Huang and His Empire (221 BC—206 BC)
3. The Silk Road in the Han Dynasty (206 BC—220 AD)
4. The Tang Dynasty (618—907)
5. Genghis Khan, Kublai Khan and the Yuan Dynasty (1271—1368)
6. Zheng He's Voyages to the Western Oceans (1405—1433)
7. Dr. Sun Yat-sen and the Beginning of the Republic of China (1911)
8. The Founding of the People's Republic of China (1949)
9. The Reform and Opening-up (1978—present day)
10. Important Recent Events

Let's find out

- Who are believed to be the ancestors of the Chinese people?
- Who are some notable figures in Chinese history?
- What are some of the most famous historical events in Chinese history?
- What has happened since China's reform and opening-up?

Let's watch a video

Let's find out more

1. The Ancestors of the Chinese People (before 2070 BC)

- Why do Chinese people call themselves the descendants of Yandi and Huangdi?

Over 4000 years ago, many clans and tribes lived in the Yellow River Valley. The two most important tribes were led by Huangdi (the Yellow Emperor) and Yandi (the Yan Emperor).

There was a warlike tribe named Jiuli whose leader was Chiyou. The Jiuli attacked Yandi's tribe. Yandi lost several battles to the Jiuli and asked Huangdi for help.

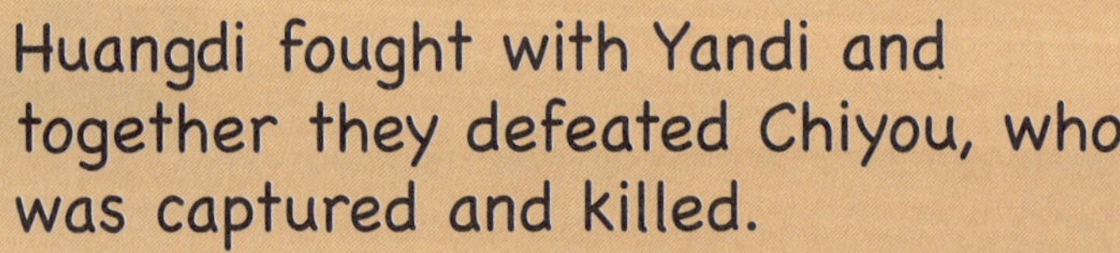

Huangdi fought with Yandi and together they defeated Chiyou, who was captured and killed.

Huangdi then ruled over all the tribes of the Central Plains. They called themselves the Huaxia people, and they were the ancestors of the Chinese people. This is why Chinese people call themselves the descendants of Yandi and Huangdi.

Activity time

Capturing Chiyou

Use the keyboard to lead Huangdi's soldiers through the maze to capture Chiyou. Try to collect as many weapons as you can on your way and do it as quickly as possible.

2. Qin Shi Huang and His Empire (221 BC–206 BC)

- Who was the first emperor of ancient China?
- What did he do whilst he was on the throne?

Before the establishment of the Qin Dynasty in 221 BC, China was a land of many states, and Qin was one of them. There were numerous wars among the states. Historically this was the Warring States Period (475 BC-221 BC)

After King Yingzheng came into power in 221 BC, Qin united the whole China.

Yingzheng called himself the First Emperor and was known as Qin Shi Huang. He is mainly remembered for:

- Building the Great Wall.

- Introducing a standard system of length, volume, weight, and currency.

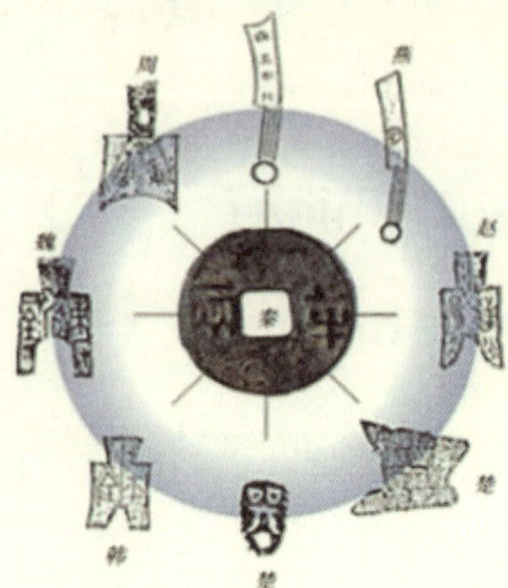

- Burying Terracotta Warriors in his tomb.

Draw a Terracotta Warrior using this grid.

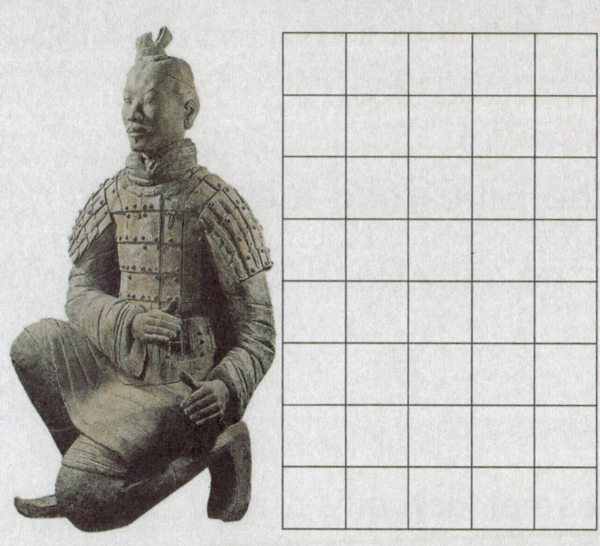

Lady Meng Jiang Weeping over the Great Wall

Follow-up activities

1. Answer the following questions:
   - How did Lady Meng Jiang and Wan Xiliang know each other?
   - What happened on their wedding night?
   - Did Lady Meng Jiang find her husband in the end?
2. Draw pictures of the story.
3. Retell the story in your own words.

3. The Silk Road in the Han Dynasty (206 BC–220 AD)

- What does the Silk Road mean?
- Where does the Silk Road begin and where does it end?

The Silk Road was not actually a road. It was not paved. It was not even a single route.

The Silk Road was a name given to any trade route that linked China to countries in Central and West Asia, Africa and Europe.

The Silk Road in China was started by Zhang Qian during the Han Dynasty (206 BC-220 AD). It began in Xi'an in China, went through Middle Asia and ended at the Mediterranean Sea.

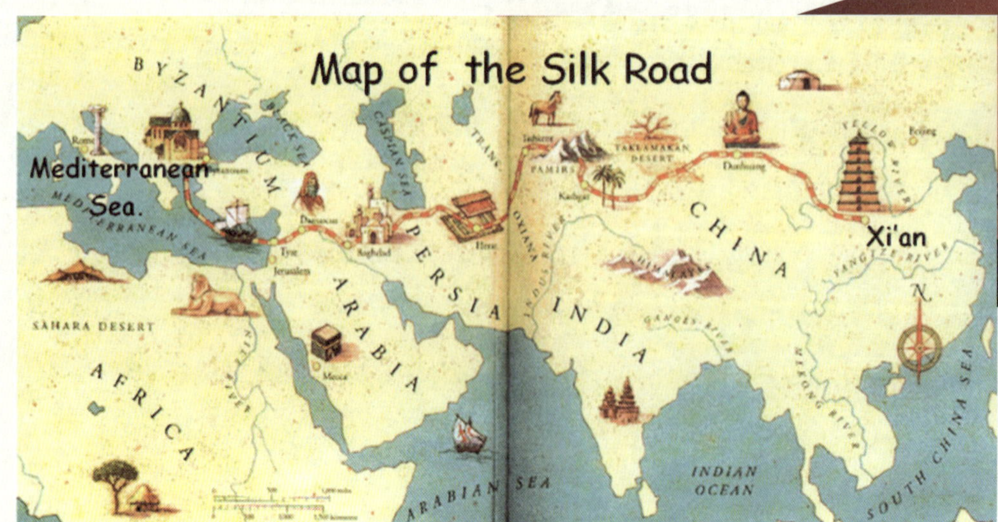

Do you know?
Camels were commonly used on the Silk Road to carry goods.

Activity time

IMAGINE you are a merchant in ancient China. You plan to travel from China to Rome to trade goods. CHOOSE what you would take with you from the items below and GIVE your reasons for choosing these items:

A. camel

B. china

C. compass and map

D. spices

E. water bottle

F. silk

MAKE a list of any other things that you would like to take with you and EXPLAIN why.

---

4. The Tang Dynasty (618–907)

- Why was the Tang Dynasty considered the most prosperous in ancient China?
- Have there been any empresses in China's history?

Du Fu

The Tang Dynasty was founded in 618 and ended in 907. It is generally regarded as a Golden Age in China's history because it was both prosperous and socially progressive.

The Tang Dynasty is also considered to be the greatest period for Chinese poetry. Two of China's most famous poets, Li Bai and Du Fu, lived during this dynasty.

The first and only empress in Chinese history, Wu Zetian, lived during the Tang Dynasty.

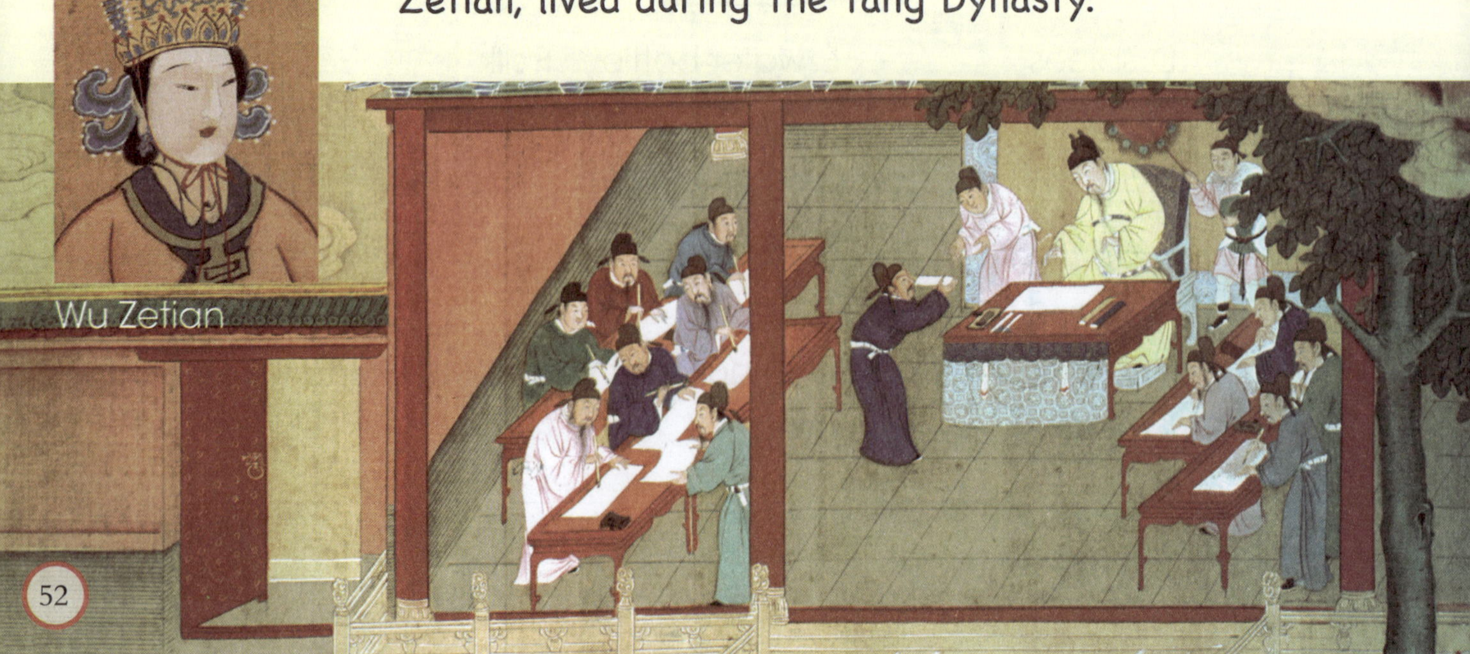
Wu Zetian

1. Learn a poem by Li Bai: Thoughts on a Still Night.

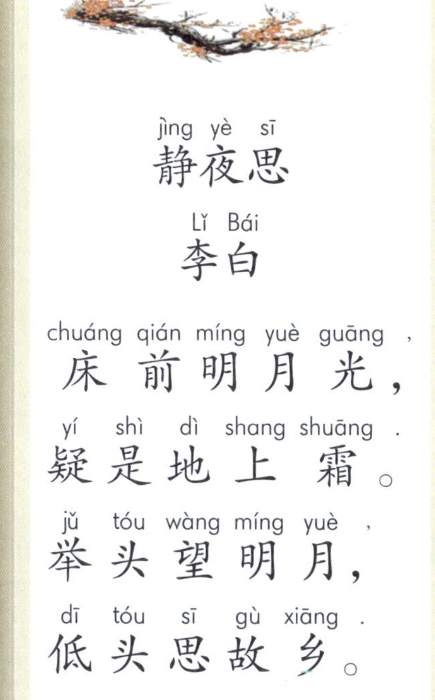

jìng yè sī
静夜思

Lǐ Bái
李白

chuáng qián míng yuè guāng ,
床前明月光，

yí shì dì shang shuāng .
疑是地上霜。

jǔ tóu wàng míng yuè ,
举头望明月，

dī tóu sī gù xiāng .
低头思故乡。

Thoughts on a Still Night
by Li Bai

Before my bed, the moon
is shining bright,

I think that it is frost
upon the ground.

I raise my head and look
at the bright moon,

I lower my head and
think of home.

Follow-up activities

1) Discuss:
   - When did Li Bai write this poem?
   - What was the weather like when he was writing this poem?
   - How was he feeling when he wrote this poem?
2) Write a poem in Li Bai's style to express your feelings.

Li Bai

2. During the Tang Dynasty, fashion was very important. USE your imagination and design a costume for a Tang lady. DRAW your picture on a piece of paper.

3. LISTEN to the story of the Monkey King. USE your imagination and PAINT the face of the Monkey King.

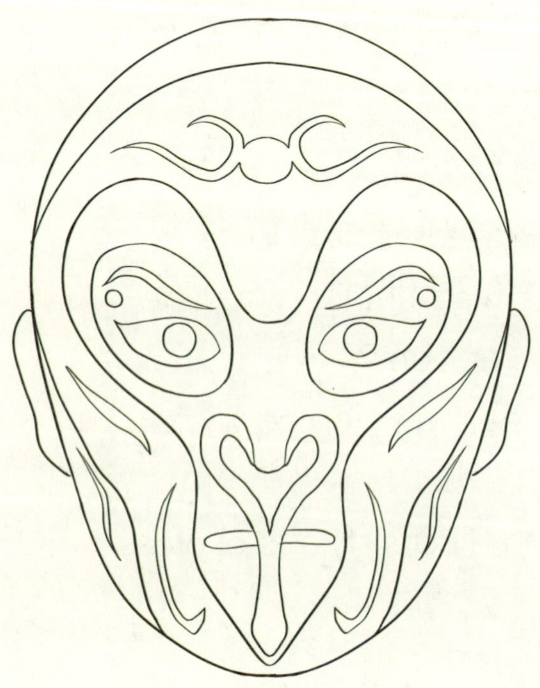

5. Genghis Khan, Kublai Khan and the Yuan Dynasty (1271–1368)

- Has China been invaded by foreign tribes?
- Who was Genghis Khan?
- Who was Kublai Khan?

The Mongols were the first foreign tribe to have conquered China and established their rule in China.

The Mongols were a tribe of nomadic people who lived in Mongolia. They were primarily herdsmen and traders, who herded sheep and traded horses.

During the 13th and 14th centuries, the Mongol Empire became very strong and became the largest empire in the history of the world. In the early 1270s, the Mongols began to invade China.

In 1271, the Mongols established the Yuan Dynasty. In 1279, they crushed the Han Chinese with Kublai Khan as the first emperor.

Genghis Khan

- A great Mongol leader
- One of the world's greatest conquerors

Kublai Khan

- Genghis Khan's grandson
- Conqueror of China
- First emperor of the Yuan Dynasty

Do you know?
Khan is a title given to rulers or other important figures in some Asian countries.

The Yuan Dynasty ruled over a vast area which was much bigger than today's China, including some parts of Europe.

Map of the Yuan Dynasty

Map of China Today (shown in red)

IMAGINE you are part of a Mongol tribe, WRITE a diary entry about a day in your life.

Bow and Arrows

Get a go at this game and score high!

6. Zheng He's Voyages to the Western Oceans (1405-1433)

- Who was Zheng He?
- Why did he sail to the Western Oceans?
- Where did he go on his voyages?

The Ming Dynasty ruled China from 1368 to 1644. In order to expand and build relationships with other countries in the world, Emperor Yongle sent Zheng He, a navy commander, on a mission to the Western Oceans, now known as the Indian Ocean.

Zheng He sailed to the Western Oceans seven times between 1405 and 1433. The first voyage was made from Nanjing on the 11th day of the 7th lunar month in 1405. Zheng He commanded a fleet of 208 ships, loaded with silk, porcelain, tea, spices and other goods. It was a magnificent fleet with a crew of over 27,500 people, the largest in the world at the time. The fleet travelled to Sumatra, Ceylon, India and even sailed as far as the eastern coast of Africa and the Red Sea.

Six similar voyages were made over the following 28 years. They took place decades before Christopher Columbus' adventure to America in 1492.

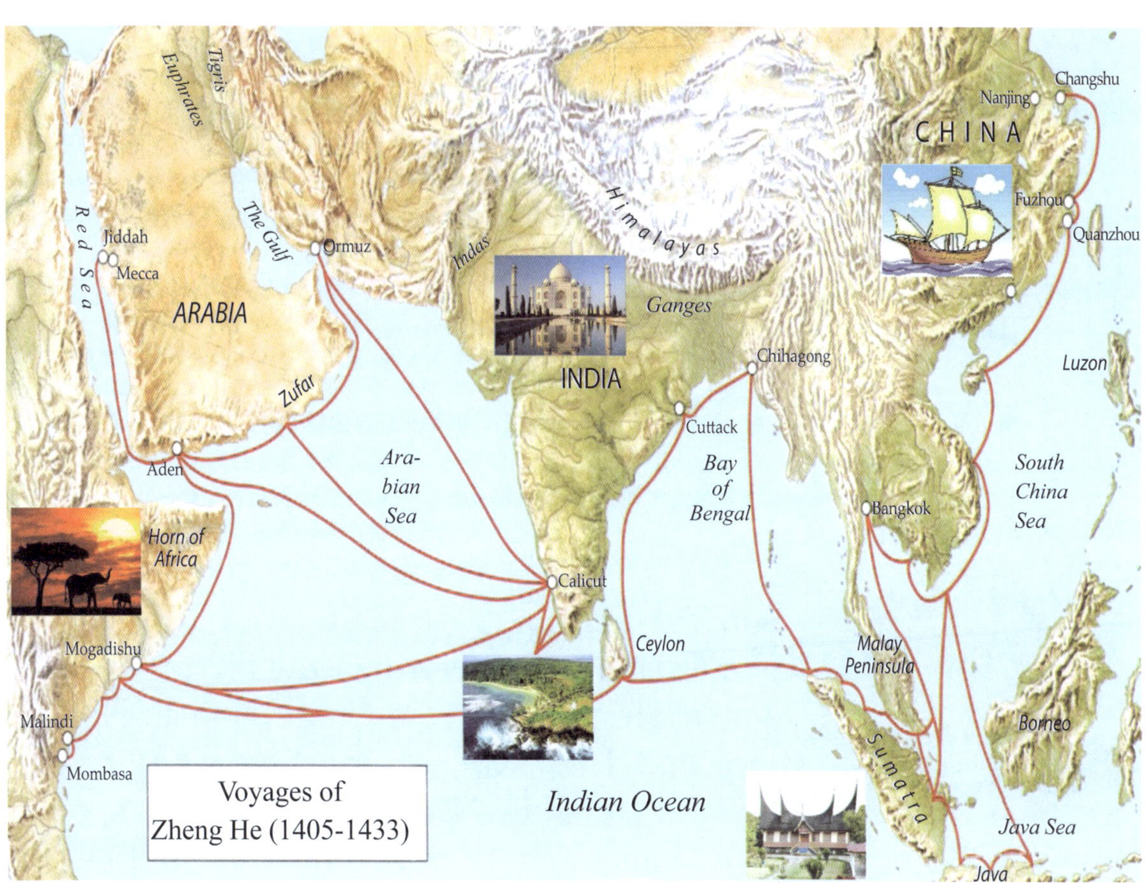

Sailing to the Western Oceans

In this game, you will travel to the Western Oceans in Zheng He's fleet. At each stop Zheng He and his sailors will trade with the local people. You must choose the right gifts to offer the local people. Choosing wisely will enable you to continue your journey.

7. Dr. Sun Yat-sen and the Beginning of the Republic of China

- Who was Dr. Sun Yat-sen?
- What were his main achievements?

Sun Yat-sen, born in 1866, was the son of a farmer. He lived in Hawaii for many years before he studied medicine in Hong Kong, and then worked in Macao, Guangzhou and Honolulu. During these years, Sun Yat-sen became interested in politics and became a political leader in China.

Under his influence, the army turned against the Qing rulers. The Qing Dynasty collapsed and the Republic of China was established in 1911. This was known as the Revolution of 1911.

READ the questions and FIND the answers. Then colour each pair in the same colour.

Did Sun Yat-sen work in Macao after graduating?

What happened in 1911?

When was Sun Yat-sen born?

Was Sun Yat-sen's father a teacher?

Yes, he did.

He was born in 1866.

No, he was a farmer.

The Republic of China was established.

8. The Founding of the People's Republic of China (1949)

- When was the People's Republic of China founded?
- Who was Chairman Mao?
- Where is the capital city of the People's Republic of China?
- What does China's national flag look like?

On October the 1st, 1949, the founding ceremony of the People's Republic of China (PRC) was held.

300,000 people gathered at Tian'anmen Square in Beijing.

Mao Zedong, the first Chairman of the PRC, standing on the Tian'anmen Gate Tower, declared to the world: "The People's Republic of China has been officially founded!"

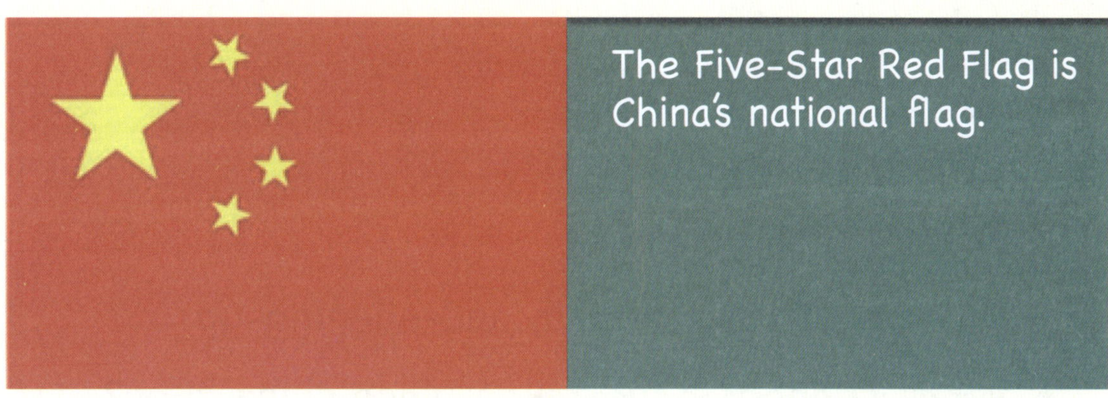

The capital city of China is Beijing.

MAKE a model of Tian'anmen Gate Tower.

9. The Reform and Opening-up (1978–present day)

- Who led China's reform and opening-up?
- What changes have taken place since then?

Deng Xiaoping — the leader of China's reform and opening-up

Great changes have taken place in China since the late 1970s, when the country underwent a political change and carried out the policy of reform and opening-up.

Here are some contrasting pictures to show the changes in China BEFORE and AFTER the reform and opening-up:

China BEFORE Reform and Opening-up		China AFTER Reform and Opening-up
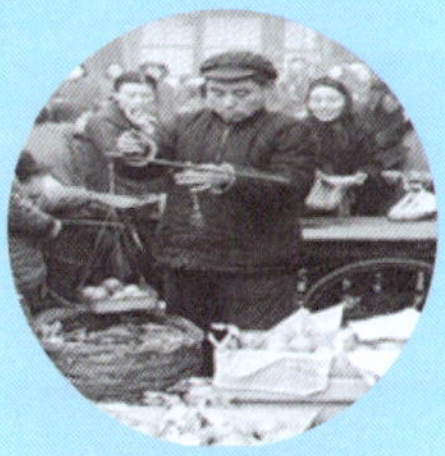	Shopping	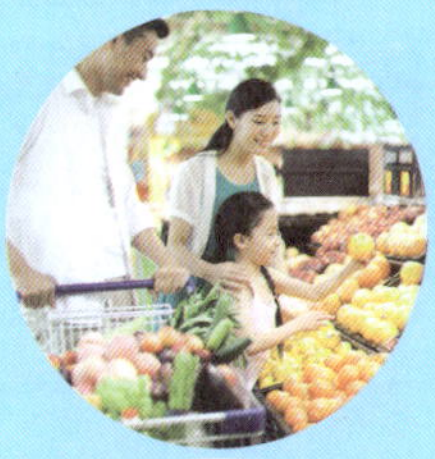
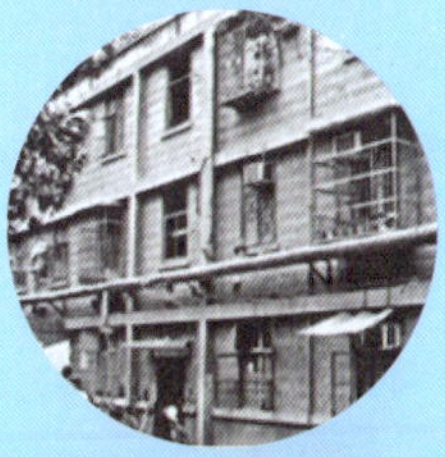	Homes	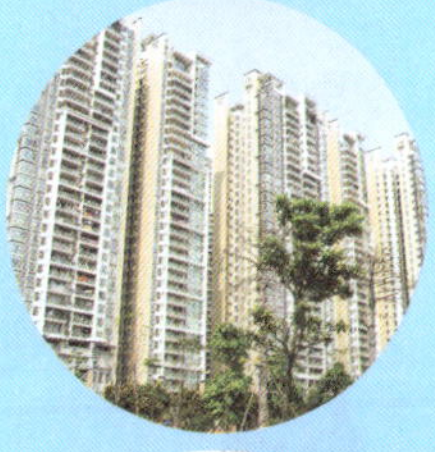
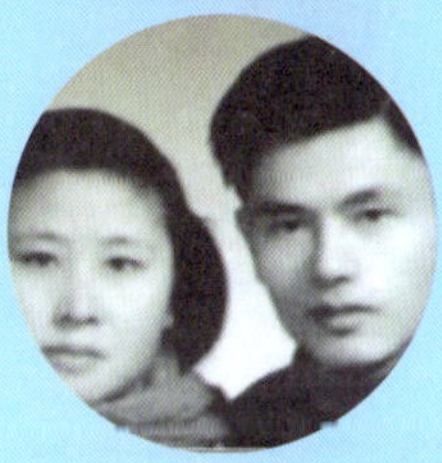	People	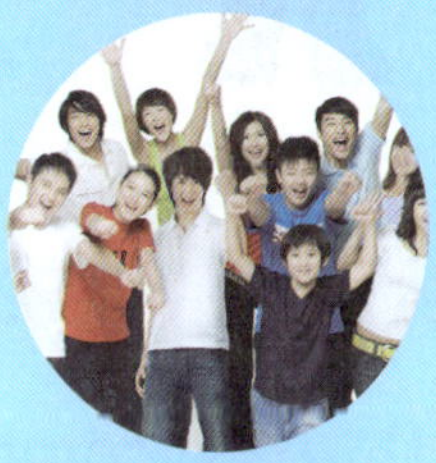
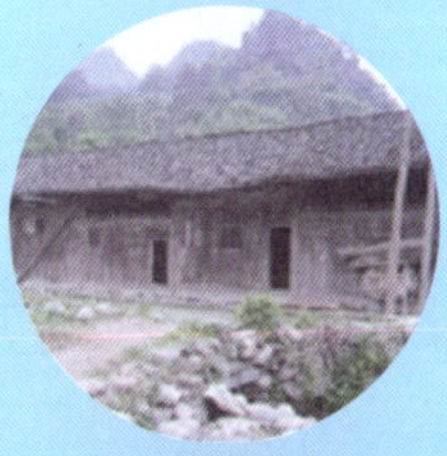	Schools	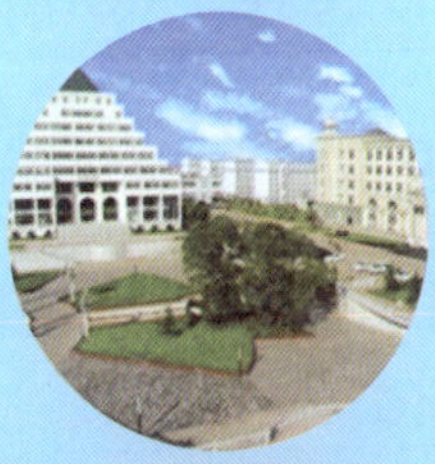
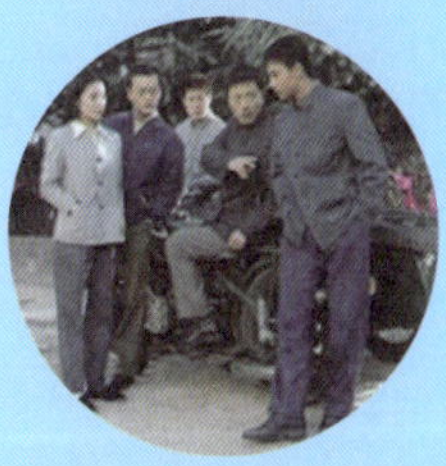	Clothes	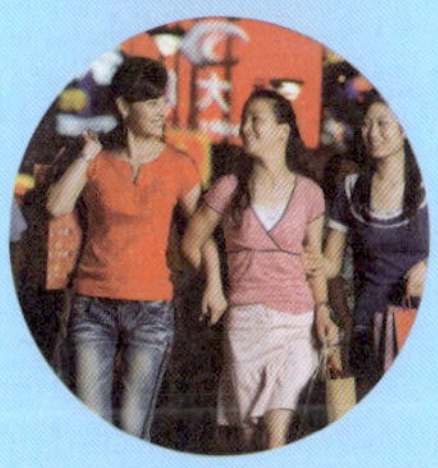

Activity time

LOOK at each pair of the pictures again and DISCUSS their differences. What changes can you see in Chinese people's lives?

10. Important Recent Events

- 2008 Beijing Olympics
- 2010 Shanghai World Expo

The 2008 Summer Olympics took place in Beijing, from August 8th to 24th in 2008.

- 11,028 athletes competed in the games.
- China was the 22nd nation to host the Olympic Games.
- It was the third time the Summer Olympic Games were held in Asia.
- The mascots: Five fuwa (Beibei, Jingjing, Huanhuan, Yingying, and Nini).

Together, their names form the sentence 北京欢迎你, or "Běijīng huānyíng nǐ," which means "Beijing welcomes you".

The Shanghai World Expo was held in Shanghai, from May 1st to October 31wt in 2010.

- The theme was "Better City, Better Life".
- 250 countries and international organisations participated.
- The Mascots were called "Haibao", meaning "treasure of the sea".

Activity time

IMAGINE you have been to China for a holiday. DESIGN a postcard and send it to your friend, showing them some scenery in China and sharing with them your experience.

Language

UNIT 4

1. Early Chinese Writing
2. Mandarin Chinese and Local Dialects
3. Chinese Writing and Pronunciation
4. Chinese Calligraphy

Let's find out

- What languages are spoken in China?
- What is the history of the Chinese language?
- How are Chinese characters written?
- What is the art of Chinese calligraphy?

Let's watch a video

1. Early Chinese Writing

- When was Chinese first written?
- What did it look like?

The very first examples of Chinese writing date to the late Shang Dynasty around 1200 BC. They were symbols cut into turtle shells and animal bones, called the oracle bone script. Samples of the oracle bone script were found at the site of the late Shang (1300 BC–1046 BC) capital near Anyang in Henan Province.

Oracle bone script

Oracle bones were usually made from pieces of ox bone or tortoise shell. However, other animal bones were also used, most notably bones from sheep, boars, horses and deer. The oracle bone script is therefore also called "shell and bone script"(Jiaguwen).

Ox bone

Tortoise shell

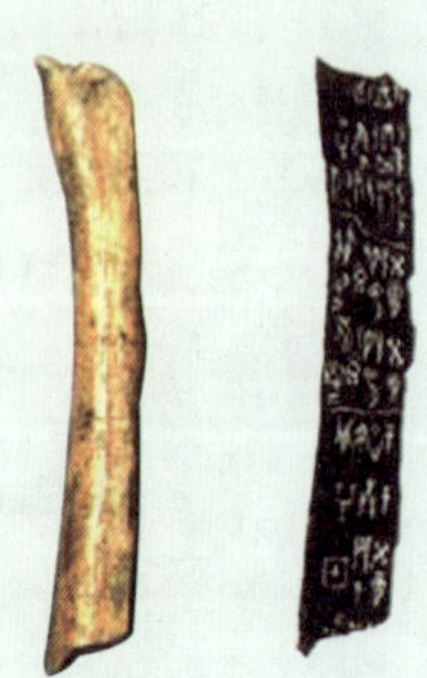

Animal ribs

Old Chinese words

In those days, old Chinese words were usually made up of one syllable. Some words were represented by symbols such as:

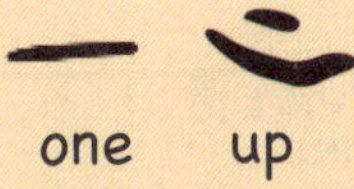

Do you know?
There are about 4000 oracle bone symbols. Today, we only know the meaning of around half of them. About 1000 oracle bone symbols are still used today.

Cang Jie Invented Words

According to legend, a man named Cang Jie invented Chinese words during the reign of the Yellow Emperor in ancient China.

Cang Jie was responsible for recording all the national affairs. At that time, there were no pens or paper, and even characters had not yet been invented. People

often tied a string to record things and they tied one knot if one thing happened.

However, Cang Jie had too many things to record, and not enough strings to record them with.

One day, Cang Jie went hunting with an elderly hunter. The hunter pointed to some traces on the ground, saying "Look, these are the footprints of the birds and beasts. Some of them are big and some small; some are deep and some shallow. These footprints have various shapes and each of them represents a different animal." Suddenly, an idea occurred to Cang Jie: Why not use different symbols to represent different things?

After that hunting trip, Cang Jie started to design symbols that could be used to represent things. Cang Jie not only used these symbols himself, but also taught other people to use them. Gradually, these symbols became widely used. Later on, the symbols were further added to and revised by many people. Eventually, they became characters, the earliest Chinese writing.

2. Mandarin Chinese and Local Dialects

- What is the official language of China?
- How many dialects are spoken in China?

Mandarin—*putonghua*

Over one billion people, about one-fifth of the world's population, speak Mandarin Chinese as their first language.

The official language of the People's Republic of China is Mandarin, also called *putonghua*. It originated in the north of the country. All Chinese children learn Mandarin in school and this is the main language used in government, education and in the media.

Mandarin is also referred to as the "northern dialect". Quite often, a person who comes from the north and another who comes from the south won't understand each other unless they speak the standard language, which is Mandarin. This is because their "dialects" (accents, specific words, expressions and tones) are totally different.

Mandarin Areas in China

Do you know?
More people speak Mandarin than any other language in the world.

For historical reasons, the dialect spoken in Hong Kong and Macao is Cantonese, although nowadays more and more people there can also speak Mandarin.

Dialects in China

The eight most common dialects spoken in China are Mandarin (i.e. *putonghua*), Wu (spoken in Shanghai, Jiangsu and Zhejiang provinces). Yue (i.e. Cantonese), Min (spoken in Fujian and Taiwan provinces), Xiang (spoken in Hunan Province), Gan (spoken in Jiangxi Province) and Hakka.

About two-thirds of the Han people are native speakers of *putonghua*. Various ethnic groups such as the Mongolian, Tibetan, Naxi, Yi, Uygur, as well as many other ethnic groups have their own native languages.

Dialects Spoken in China

Activity time

Let's LEARN Mandarin.

Nǐ hǎo.
你好。
Hello.

Zàijiàn.
再见。
Goodbye.

Xièxie.
谢谢。
Thank you.

Do you know?
The languages of Korea, Japan, Vietnam and the Philippines all include some Chinese vocabulary.

3. Chinese Writing and Pronunciation

- What does written Chinese look like?
- How many characters are there in the Chinese language?
- How are Chinese characters written?
- What is the pinyin system?

Chinese characters

Hello = 你 Nǐ 好 hǎo

In English and many other Western languages, there is an alphabet. In Chinese, there are "characters" and every Chinese character has a unique meaning and pronunciation.

Guess which one of the following characters is a Chinese character?

When you first look at Chinese characters, they may seem to be just a jumble of confusing lines. However, after you look at them for a while, you will begin to see a pattern of symbols that have individual meanings, unlike the letters of the alphabet.

How has Chinese writing developed?

Chinese is one of the oldest writing systems still in use today. As you already know, the first examples of Chinese writing were found on oracle bones. After that, Chinese writing evolved into several forms, as illustrated below:

Oracle Bone Script (Jiaguwen)	日	月	車	馬
Bronze Inscriptions (Jinwen)	日	月	車	馬
Lesser Seal (Xiaozhuan)	日	月	車	馬
Clerical Script (Lishu)	日	月	車	馬
Regular Script (Kaishu)	日	月	車	馬
Cursive Script (Caoshu)	日	月	車	馬
Running Script (Xingshu)	日	月	車	馬

There are two types of Chinese characters used in China: "simplified Chinese" and "traditional Chinese". Simplified Chinese characters are used in China's mainland. These characters were adopted in 1956, after the People's Republic of China was founded. They are also called "the modern form" of Chinese. The government developed "simplified Chinese" to make it easier for people to learn to read and write in Chinese.

simplified Chinese

Nowadays, traditional Chinese is mostly used in Hong Kong and Taiwan. As its name suggests, this is a traditional way of writing that has been used by Chinese people for thousands of years. The characters are more complicated to write.

Not every Chinese character has been simplified, only the most difficult ones. Some characters have stayed exactly the same. Generally, simplified Chinese characters have fewer strokes and are easier to write than traditional Chinese characters. For example, "dragon" in simplified Chinese is written as 龙, but in traditional Chinese is written as 龍.

traditional Chinese

Character Catcher

Use the basket to catch the falling Chinese characters.

The number of Chinese characters

The exact number of Chinese characters that have existed since the ancient times is not certain, but it is estimated that it amounts to over 90,000 characters. Only roughly 10,000 are now commonly used.

It is believed that a person needs to know about 2000 characters to be able to use Chinese in their daily lives, such as reading a newspaper, shopping and for general conversations. A university student will learn between 4000 and 5000 characters.

Many Chinese words are written with two or more characters and each character represents a syllable. You can guess the meaning of a new word by learning what each character means.

For example, the character 女 means "female"; the character 人 means "person". If we combine these two characters together as 女人, they mean "woman".

Writing Chinese characters

Chinese characters are written to fit into an imaginary square, and they are made up of a series of strokes. There are eight main strokes.

《别韦少府》李白

西出苍龙门，南登白鹿原。
欲寻商山皓，犹恋汉皇恩。
水国远行迈，仙经深讨论。
洗心向溪月，清耳敬亭猿。
筑室在人境，闭门无世喧。
多君枉高驾，赠我以微言。
交乃意气合，道因风雅存。
别离有相思，瑶瑟与金樽。

丶	"diǎn" — a simple dot.	永 寸 江 太
一	"héng" — a horizontal stroke, written from left to right.	王 一 大 千
丨	"shù" — a vertical stroke, written from top to bottom.	口 王 木 十
亅	"gōu" — a hook appended to other strokes.	永 小 心 丁
㇀	"tí" — a diagonal stroke, rising from left to right.	冰 打 地 功
丿	"piě" — a diagonal stroke, falling from right to left.	永 人 女 千
㇏	"nà" - a diagonal stroke, falling from left to right.	永 人 又 木
㇕	"héngzhé" - a turning stroke, composed of a horizontal stroke and a vertical one.	血 口 中 目

Each character is written in strokes, following a proper order. When writing characters, these eight basic rules are followed:

1. Horizontal strokes are written before vertical ones.

2. Left-falling strokes are written before right-falling ones.

3. Characters are written from top to bottom.

毛 ノ 二 三 毛

4. Characters are written from left to right.

州 丶 丿 少 州 州 州

5. If a character is framed from above, the frame is written first.

同 丨 冂 冂 同 同 同

6. If a character is framed from below, the frame is written last.

凶 丿 乂 凶 凶

7. Frames are closed last.

四 丨 冂 四 四 四

8. In a symmetrical character, the middle strokes are written first, then the side strokes.

小 亅 小 小

Writing the character "wan"

Follow-up activities

1. How many strokes are needed to write the character "wan"?
2. How many strokes does the boy think that he needs to do in order to write the character "wan"? Why does he think so?

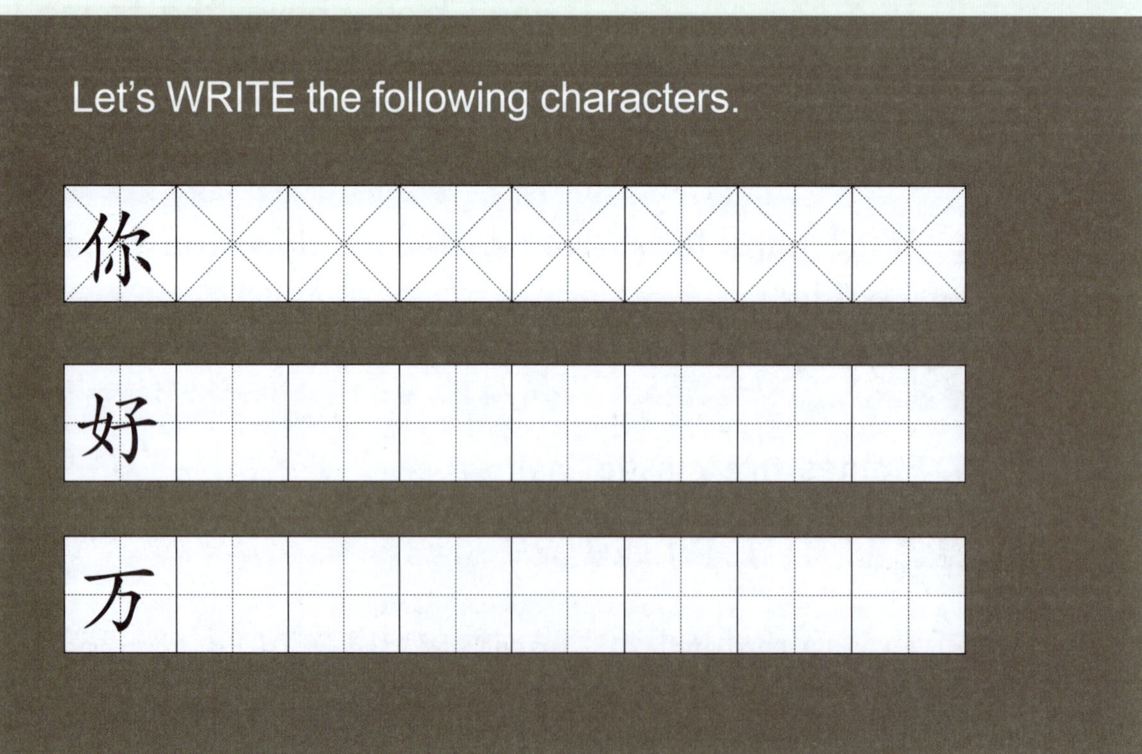

Guessing the Character's Meaning

One Chinese character will appear on the screen at a time. Guess the meaning from its shape.

The pinyin system

The pinyin system was published by the Chinese government in 1958. It is the official system used to transcribe Chinese characters into the Latin alphabet. It is used to teach Mandarin Chinese in schools and is a handy tool for many foreigners to learn Mandarin.

Initials and Finals

Pinyin in Mandarin literally means "spell sound". It spells out the sounds of the characters, making it easier for people to speak the language without having to learn as many characters. In pinyin, the pronunciation and spelling of Chinese words are given in terms of initials and finals. Nearly every Mandarin character can be spelt with exactly one initial followed by one final.

Examples: Initial + Final nǐ hǎo (你好) xièxie (谢谢)

Tones

The pinyin system also uses "tones", which are placed over letters and show us how to pronounce characters correctly. There are four tones and one neutral tone in Mandarin Chinese. Neutral tones are usually unmarked.

1. The first tone – the flat or high level tone
2. The second tone – the rising tone
3. The third tone – the falling-rising tone
4. The fourth tone – the falling tone
5. The neutral tone

Tones	Tone Marks
1st tone	ˉ
2nd tone	ˊ
3rd tone	ˇ
4th tone	ˋ

This diagram gives you an idea of how different the tones sound.

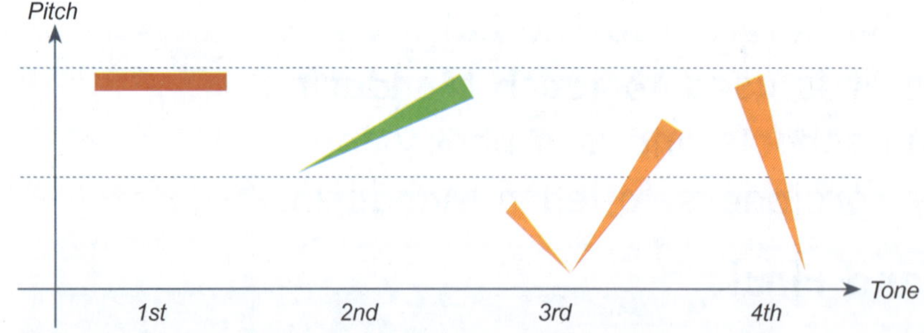

Pinyin tones are very important for people to pronounce the characters correctly. Using the wrong tone can change the meaning of a word. For example:

mā 妈 má 麻 mǎ 马 mà 骂 ma 吗

This same sound said with the five different tones respectively mean "mother", "hemp", "horse", "scold" and "a grammatical word to show a question".

When you use a computer you can use pinyin to type Chinese characters.

Dot-to-Dot Drawing

JOIN the dots by following the Chinese pinyin in the correct order.

Wǒ ài xuéxiào, ài lǎoshī, ài tóngxué.

4. Chinese Calligraphy

- What is Chinese calligraphy?
- What are the four essential tools you need to do Chinese calligraphy?
- How many styles of Chinese calligraphy are there?
- How do you practise Chinese calligraphy?

Chinese calligraphy

The word "calligraphy" means "beautiful writing". Calligraphy is both a technique for writing Chinese characters and a unique oriental art. Invented and

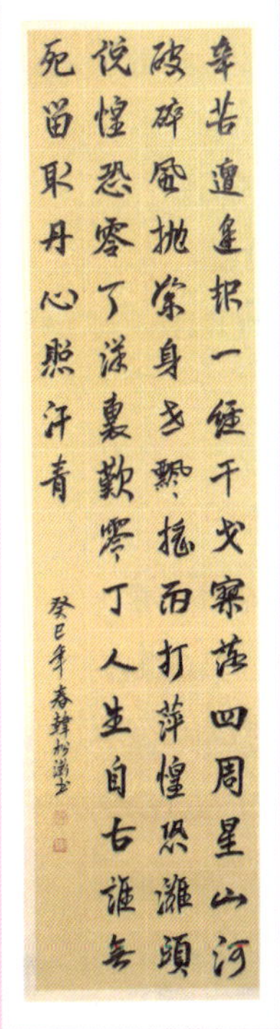

Caoshu

Kaishu

developed in China, it is a very important part of Chinese culture. It is also popular in other East Asian countries like Korea and Japan.

There are different ways of writing Chinese characters with a brush. Here are some important styles:

"Kaishu" is the main Chinese writing style, it is also called "regular script". It was first used at the end of the Han Dynasty over 1700 years ago, and is still used today.

"Caoshu", or "cursive script" as it is also known, is a more creative writing style which is popular with artists as it allows them more freedom to be creative when writing.

"Zhuanshu", also known as "seal script", is generally not used outside the art of calligraphy, as not many people can write effortlessly in this style.

"Lishu", also known as "clerical script", is a simplified version of "seal script" and very similar to the modern script.

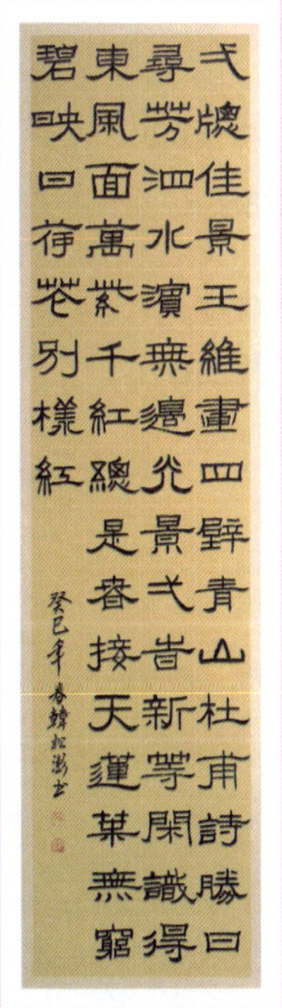

Lishu

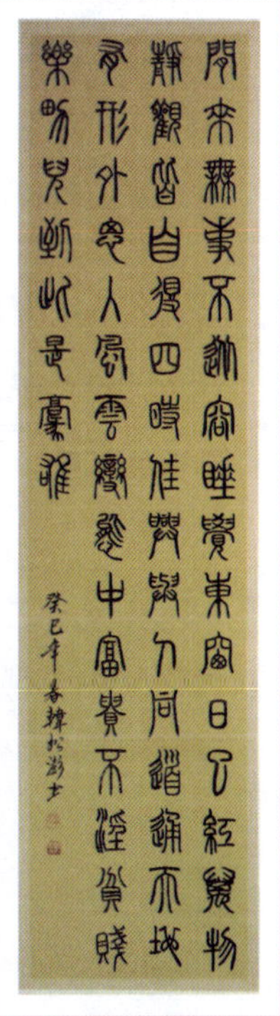

Zhuanshu

The four essential tools for calligraphy

The four important tools people use for doing Chinese calligraphy are a brush, ink, paper, and an ink-stone. These four tools are also known in China as "The Four Treasures of the Study".

Brush

The brush is the most important tool in calligraphy. The handle of the brush can be made from either bamboo, or other materials such as red sandalwood, glass, ivory, silver, or gold. The head of the brush can be made from the fur or feathers of a variety of animals, for instance, rabbits, ducks, goats, tigers or wolves. The brush itself is softer than a pencil or pen. Because of its softness, it can be used to write in light or heavy, thick or fine strokes.

One Chinese family tradition is to use the hair of a newborn baby to make the head of a writing brush to be kept and given to the child when he or she grows older.

Today, calligraphy can also be done using a pen. However, serious calligraphy artists will still use a brush.

Paper

In China, there are many special types of paper which are used for calligraphy. However, Xuan paper is considered the best to use since it is soft, very fine, and good for writing on with a brush.

Ink or ink-stick

Calligraphy ink is made from a special ink-stick. The ink-stick must be rubbed with water on an ink-stone to produce a black liquid. Much cheaper, bottled, liquid inks are now available, although learning to rub the ink-stick is an essential part of calligraphy. Traditionally, Chinese calligraphy is only done in black ink, but modern calligraphers sometimes use other colours.

Ink-stone

An ink-stone is used to grind the solid ink-stick by adding water into liquid ink and is then used as a container for the ink. For serious calligraphers, a good ink-stone is as important as the quality of the ink. An ink-stone can affect the quality and texture of the ink.

Other tools for calligraphy

Calligraphy artists use more than just the "Four Treasures" to write.

The other "treasures" include brush-holder, brush-hanger, paperweights, brush-rinsing pot, seal and seal-ink.

Beginners need to choose their four tools carefully before they start to do calligraphy, and then take good care of them after using them.

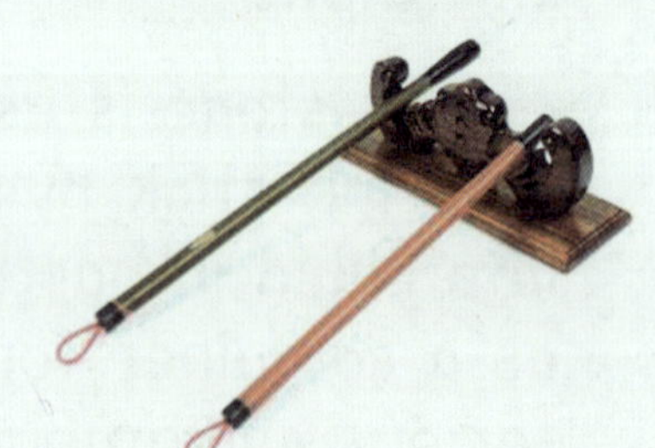

Do you know?

Lessons in basic calligraphy are part of the school curriculum in China.

You can choose to study calligraphy as a special subject at university.

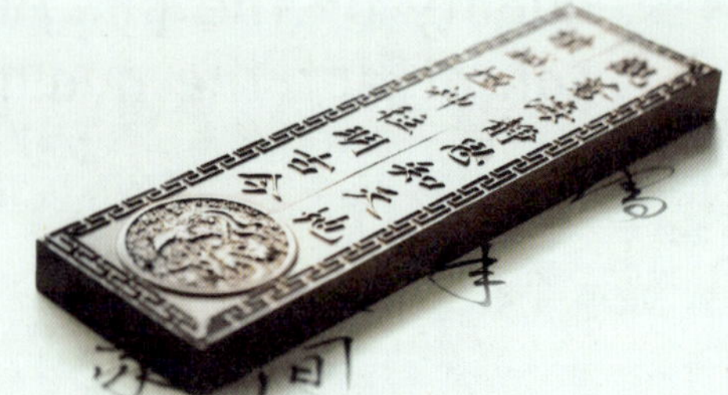

The Magic Paintbrush

Follow-up activities

1. How did Ma Liang come across the magic paintbrush?
2. How "magic" was the paintbrush?
3. What did the landlord ask Ma Liang to draw when he heard about the magic paintbrush? Did Ma Liang agree? What happened then?
4. Can you use "golden mountain", "ocean", "ship", "wind" and "sail" as the key words and retell the last part of the story when Ma Liang was sent to draw pictures for the landlord?

1. WRITE this character in a correct order of strokes.

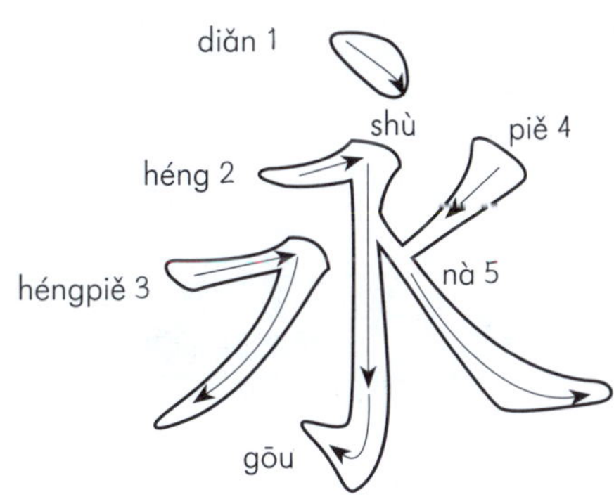

2. Let's LEARN to be a calligrapher

1) Prepare your brush.

To practise Chinese calligraphy, you must first learn the proper way to hold a calligraphy brush. Always hold the brush firmly and keep it straight and vertical to the desk. Do not hold the brush at an angle.

2) Prepare your ink.

Place a little water in the ink-stone.

Use your ink-stick to make ink by rubbing it on the stone in a circular motion until you have the right shade of black you want.

Chinese Ink-stone and Ink-stick

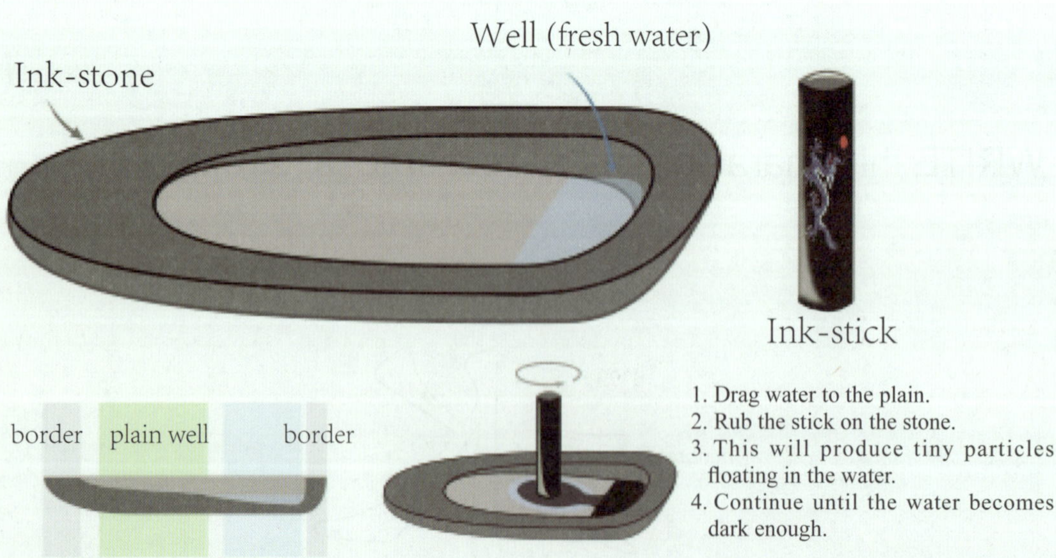

1. Drag water to the plain.
2. Rub the stick on the stone.
3. This will produce tiny particles floating in the water.
4. Continue until the water becomes dark enough.

3. WRITE the numbers 1-10 in Chinese in the following squares.

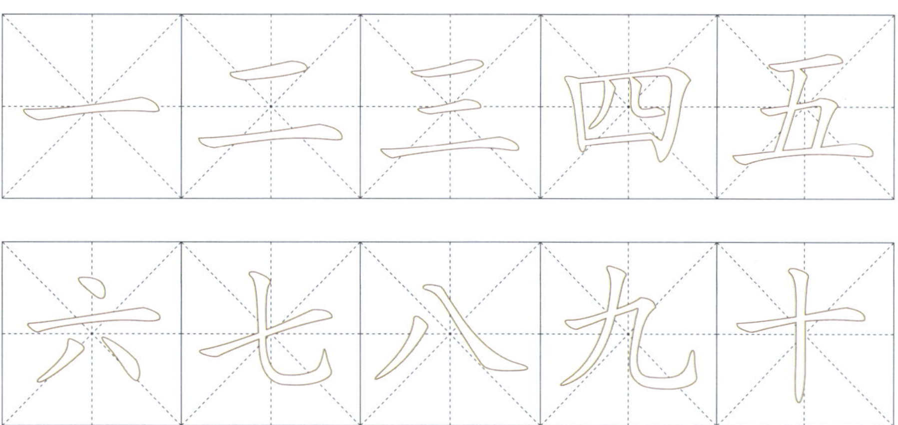

Identifying Stroke Order

Tell whether each character is written in a correct order of strokes.

Education

UNIT 5

1. Confucius
2. Schools for Boys and Girls in Ancient China
3. The Imperial Examination
4. Education in China Today
5. The National College Entrance Examination

Let's find out

- How were people educated in ancient China?
- How have schools in China changed?
- What are schools like in China today?

Let's watch a video

1. Confucius

- Who was Confucius?
- Why is he important?

Confucius

Confucius (551 BC–479 BC) was a great educator and thinker in ancient China. He lived about 2500 years ago, in a time called the Spring and Autumn Period (770 BC–476 BC).

Confucius was an influential educator in Chinese history and the first to argue that everyone should have an equal right to education. He set up private schools and taught as many as 3000 students.

Confucius was a social thinker. He believed that the rulers of the country should be kind to their people and that they should rule on the basis of virtue not force.

Over the centuries, Confucius' thoughts have had an enormous influence in China as well as in many other countries in Asia, particularly in Japan, South Korea and Vietnam.

To date, these countries still hold a traditional Confucius memorial ceremony every year.

Confucius' works have been studied by many scholars throughout the world and translated into many languages.

Confucian Thoughts

The teachings of Confucius were recorded after his death in a book called the *Analects*. This book has become a classic for generations of Chinese people, and what he said has become the golden rules.

Confucius Sayings

"Among any street with three people walking together, I will find something to learn from them."

三人行必
有我师焉

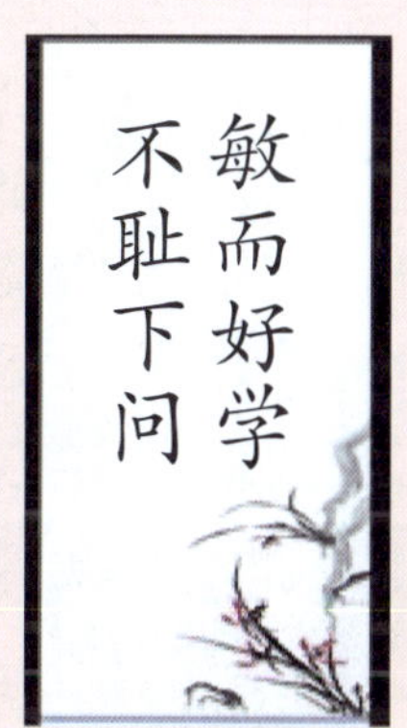

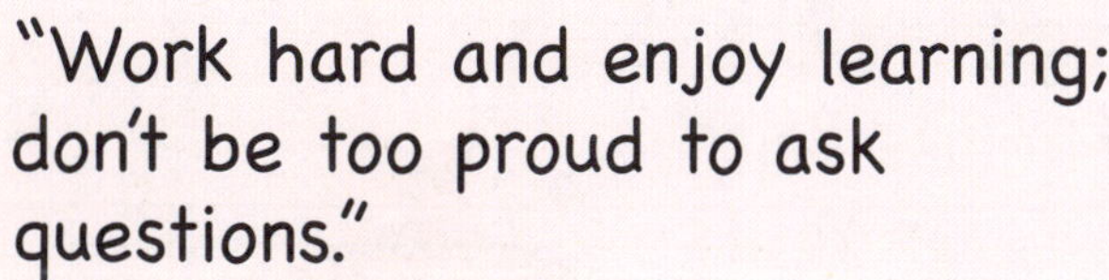

"Work hard and enjoy learning; don't be too proud to ask questions."

"Don't do to others what you don't want done to you."

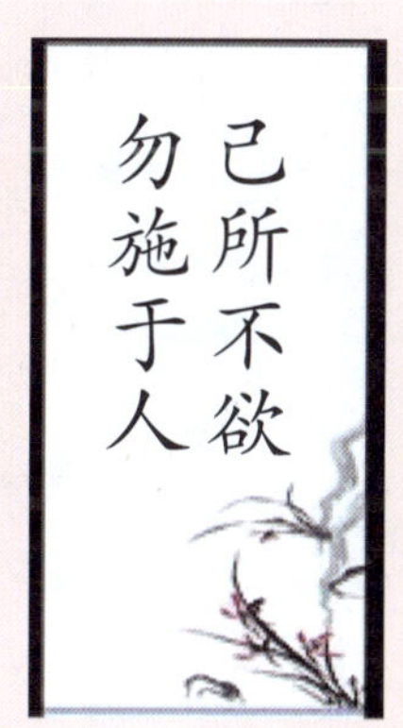

A Child Worth Teaching

Follow-up activities:

1. Here is the beginning of the story. Can you fill in the missing information?

During the Qin Dynasty in ancient China, there was a young boy named Zhang Liang. He was intelligent and hard-working, always ready to help others. He wished that he could become somebody important when he grew up, so that he could do a lot of good for people.

One day, as he was ________, he saw ______coming towards him from the other end of the bridge. As the old man came closer, Zhang Liang was able to see that the old man was wearing __________, and his shoes were worn out and dirty. Zhang Liang greeted the old man with a polite "Hello!" and walked on, but a moment later, he heard a voice shouting from behind, " __________!" Zhang Liang turned back, and saw the old man slowly __________ and threw them over the bridge,

then said, " ______!" Although Zhang Liang felt confused and annoyed, he still did as the old man told him to do, thinking that at least he should obey the old man.

When Zhang Liang handed over ______, the old man demanded, calmly, " ______!" Zhang Liang patiently put the shoes on the old man's feet and was about to take leave when the old man said to him, smilingly: "You are a good boy. ______ . I think you are a child worth teaching. ______ if you come to meet me, on this same spot, ______." Then the old man walked away.

……

2. Did the old man give Zhang Liang what he promised the second time they met?

____

3. What did the old man give Zhang Liang in the end?

____

____

____

2. Schools for Boys and Girls in Ancient China

- Did boys and girls go to school in ancient China?
- What was school like in ancient China?
- What did people learn at school at that time?

Most children in ancient China never got a chance to go to school. Only children from very rich families could get an education, and only boys were sent to school.

Starting from the late 15th century, girls from very rich families began to learn to read and write. However, it was not until the 19th century that girls were allowed to attend "girls only" schools.

Schools in ancient China

Most schools in ancient China were fairly small; some had only one teacher for the whole school. Most schools were in temples.

Children had to work very hard at school. They studied long hours, even on weekends. They sat upright on stools or benches, in front of the teacher, who sat on a chair.

Private schools called "Shuyuan" (Academies) began to bloom during the Song Dynasty (960—1279). These were schools for able and talented children.

In 1862, the first Western style school opened in Beijing and was named "Jingshi Tongwenguan" (a college funded by the Qing government to train foreign language talents).

In 1864, the first Western style middle school for girls was opened in Beijing and was called Birdgman Girls' School.

Four Books and *Five Classics*

School children in ancient China had to learn page after page of knowledge from the Confucian classics. These were based on the *Four Books* and *Five Classics*.

The *Four Books* are:

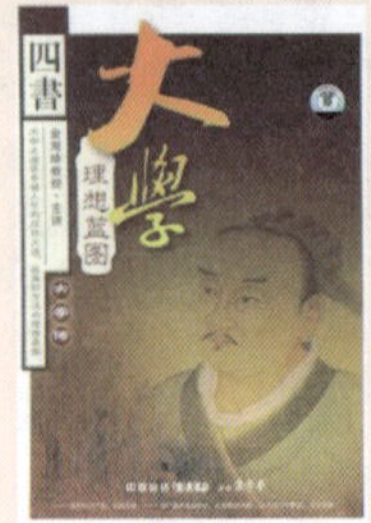

Great Learning

Doctrine of the Mean

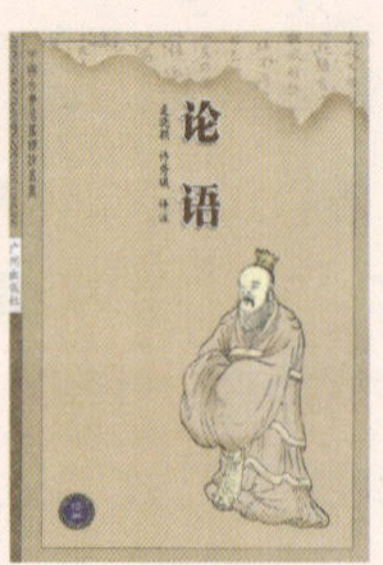

Analects

Mencius

The *Five Classics* are:

Classic of Poetry

Classic of Changes

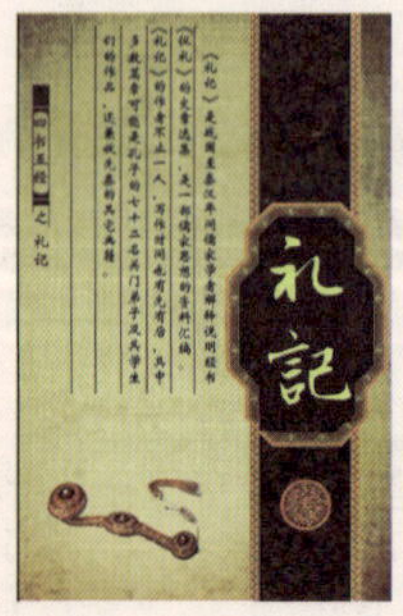

Book of Rites

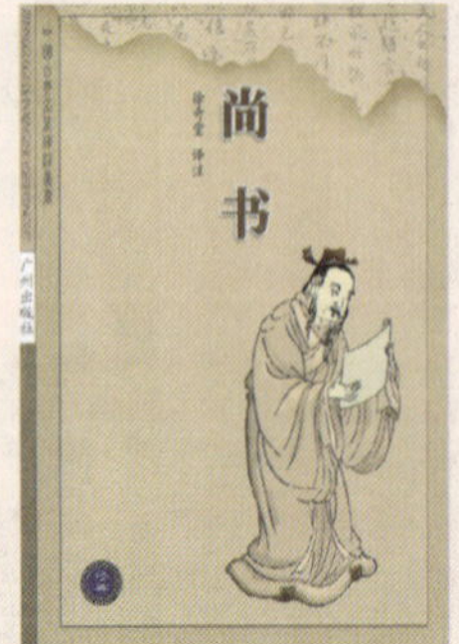

Book of Documents

Spring and Autumn Annals

These classics trained young people in the rules of society and government. They also taught young people how to behave.

In addition to memorising Confucius classics, students learnt to write essays and poetry, and to paint. There were not any mathematics or science lessons.

1. WHAT can you FIND in this classroom? Can you LABEL them?

2. Here are two pictures of a classroom in ancient China. Can you FIND the differences between them? CLICK on the differences you find.

3. The Imperial Examination

- When were examinations first introduced?
- What was in the examinations?
- Why were the examinations important?

China is said to be the first country in the world to introduce an official exam. It was introduced during the Sui Dynasty (581-618) and developed further in the Tang and Song dynasties. It gradually evolved into the structured Imperial Examination System that had lasted for over 1300 years, until 1905, when the Qing Dynasty put an end to it.

There were ranks in the examination system, and the candidates were tested on their essay writing abilities, their knowledge of the Confucian classics, and their skill in calligraphy and painting. They competed in four major rounds of examinations, starting from the county level and going all the way up to the national level. The final round of the examination took place in the royal court in the presence of the emperor, who acted as the examiner.

The four rounds of the Imperial Examination

Top:

Palace Examination

3rd round:

Metropolitan Examination

2nd round:

Provincial Examination

1st round:

Local Examination

For centuries, imperial governments would select their officials from the ranks of the successful candidates in the examinations.

Many historians thought that this examination system provided a relatively fair chance for ordinary people to compete for higher positions in the government.

The Imperial Examination took place every three years, and the process could last for one to two years. The candidates had to travel from different places to the capital city; some of them came from thousands of miles away.

Do you know?
Empress Wu Zetian of the Tang Dynasty asked the candidates questions herself during the imperial examination in the monarch hall. This started the tradition of "interview".

Fan Jin Passing the Imperial Examinations

Follow-up activities

Here are some illustrations of the story. Write a few lines for each of them, and then retell the story in your own words.

The Imperial Examination

You are travelling from a small village to the capital to sit the Imperial Examination. You will have to pass four rounds of examinations. In each round you will be asked at least three questions. Click the right answers to move on.

4. Education in China Today

- When do children in China begin schooling?
- How long do they stay in school?
- What subjects do children learn in school?
- Do they have to sit any examinations?

The Education System Today

Children in China start school at the age of six or seven. They spend six years in primary school and then three years in junior high school. These are the nine years of basic education that, by law, all children in China have to receive.

After finishing junior high school, most pupils go on to senior high school, where they study for another three years. However, some pupils choose to continue studying at vocational schools, where they learn a particular skill or trade.

Higher education in China lasts for at least four years for a Bachelor's Degree, and then another two to three years for a Master's Degree. Those who continue on to a Doctorate Degree need to study for another three to six years.

Education

The Education System in China

Age	Level of Education	Compulsory or Not
18-22	university or college	no
15-18	senior high school or vocational school	no
12-15	junior high school	yes
6-12	primary school	

The Chinese Nine-year Compulsory Education Law guarantees the right for all school-aged children (boys and girls) to receive at least nine years of education.

Primary Schools

Children in primary schools start to learn Chinese, arithmetic, and English. These are the three most important subjects in the curriculum.

They also learn music, art, science, history and geography. There are also physical education lessons and moral education lessons for everyone.

The children can also join after-school clubs. Although they are young, primary school children take turns to tidy and clean their classrooms after school.

Music Club

Dance Club

Painting Club

Cooking Lessons

Beijing Opera Club

Kungfu Club

1. Let's LEARN a Chinese song —— Find Your Friend

Do you know?

In 1949, when the People's Republic of China was founded, a survey showed that 85% of China's population didn't know how to read and write. Nowadays, over 85% of people in China have received at least nine years of basic education.

2. Let's experience a day in a Chinese primary school

7:45 am-8:00 am
National Flag Raising Ceremony

8:00 am-12:00 am Morning Classes

9:15 am Morning Exercise

12:00 am-2:00 pm Lunch Break

2:00 pm-4:00pm Afternoon Classes

3:00 pm Eye Massage

4:00 pm-5:00 pm After School Clubs

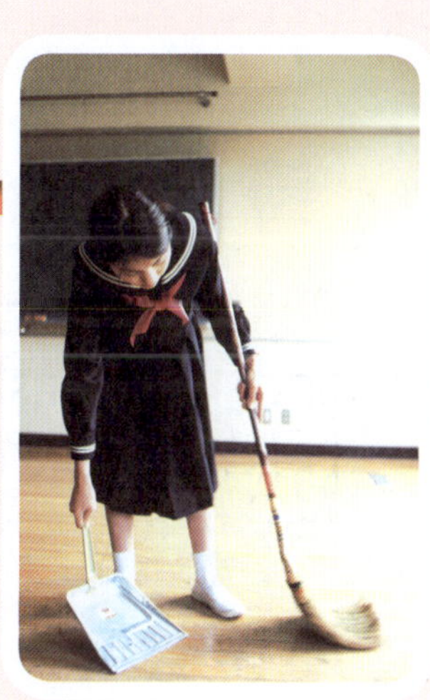

After-school Classroom Cleaning

3. Let's DO morning exercise and eye exercise.

High Schools in China

Junior high school students continue to learn Chinese, Maths and English, but they branch out when they reach senior high school into either the humanities or sciences. Each group has their separate curriculum.

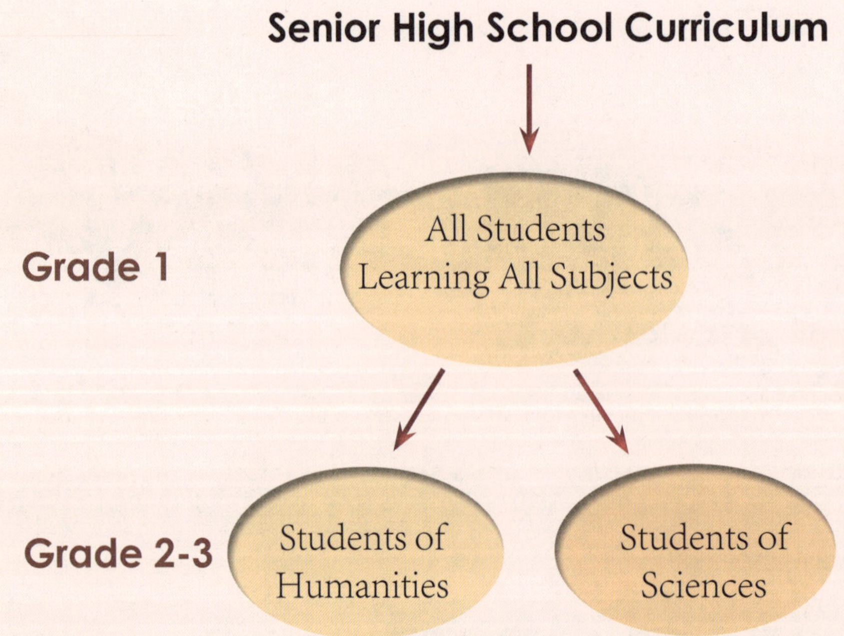

Both groups of students work very hard, especially in their final year of senior high school, because they have to compete in the College Entrance Examinations.

A Day in a Chinese High School

Normally, high school students arrive at school at around 7:00 am to 7:30 am every morning. The students are required to hand in homework to their tutors before 8:00 am. Lessons begin at 8:00 am and a session usually lasts for 45 minutes. The students have a 10-15 minute break after every lesson. All the students gather to do morning exercise on the playground every day at around 9:15 to 9:30 am. The lunch break starts at 12:00 am. In the afternoon, lessons usually start at 2:00 pm. There are various after school clubs every afternoon. In their final year, some students will attend night study at school from 7:00 pm to 9:00 pm.

7:00 am – 7:45 am Early Morning Reading

8:00 am – 11:50 am Morning Classes

9:15 am – 9:30 am Mid-session Exercise

12:00 am – 2:00 pm Lunch Break

2:00 pm – 5:00 pm Afternoon Sessions and Clubs

7:00 pm – 9:00 pm Evening Study

Education

Activity time

Let's MAKE a shuttlecock and PLAY. You will need:

- feathers
- a piece of round metal with a hole in the centre
- a small piece of cloth
- a piece of string

1

2

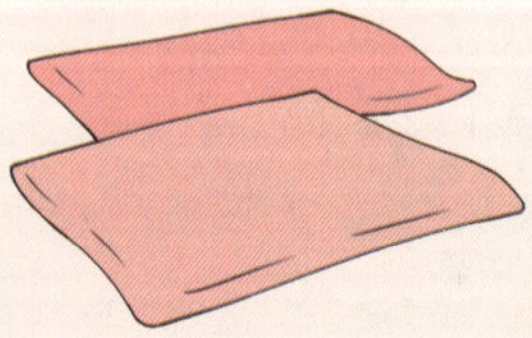

3

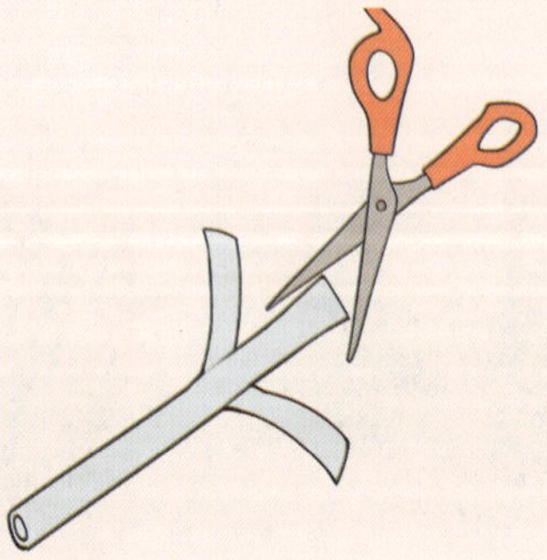

4

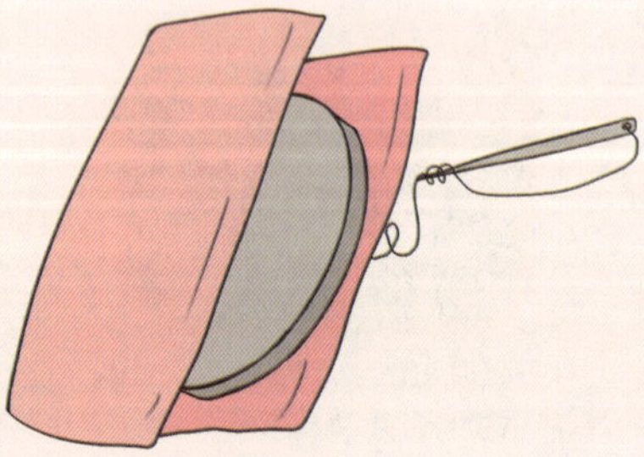

5

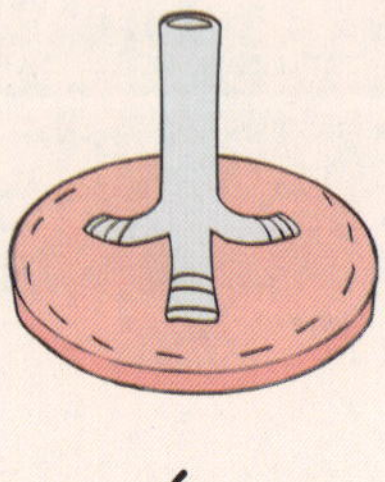

6

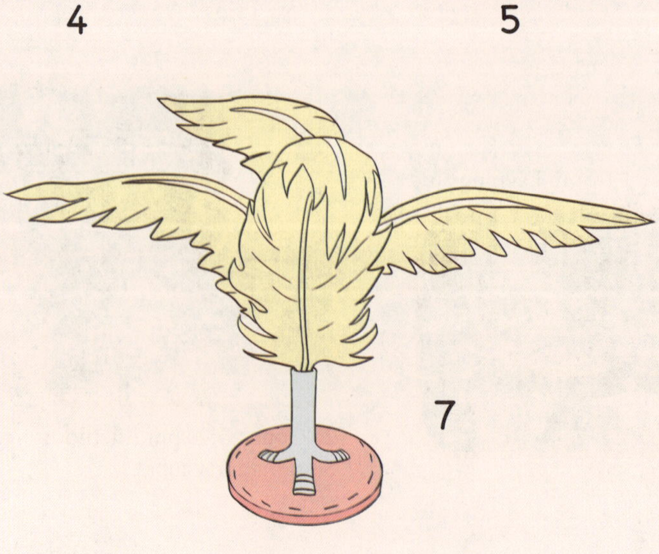

7

5. The National College Entrance Examination

- When do students sit the National College Entrance Examination?
- What is in the examination?

The National College Entrance Examination is a two-day test that students have to sit to enter university. It is a national event that takes place on fixed dates in early June every year, and students across the country take the examination on the same date at the same time.

All candidates sit an examination in Chinese, Maths and English and then an examination in their own choice of humanities or science.

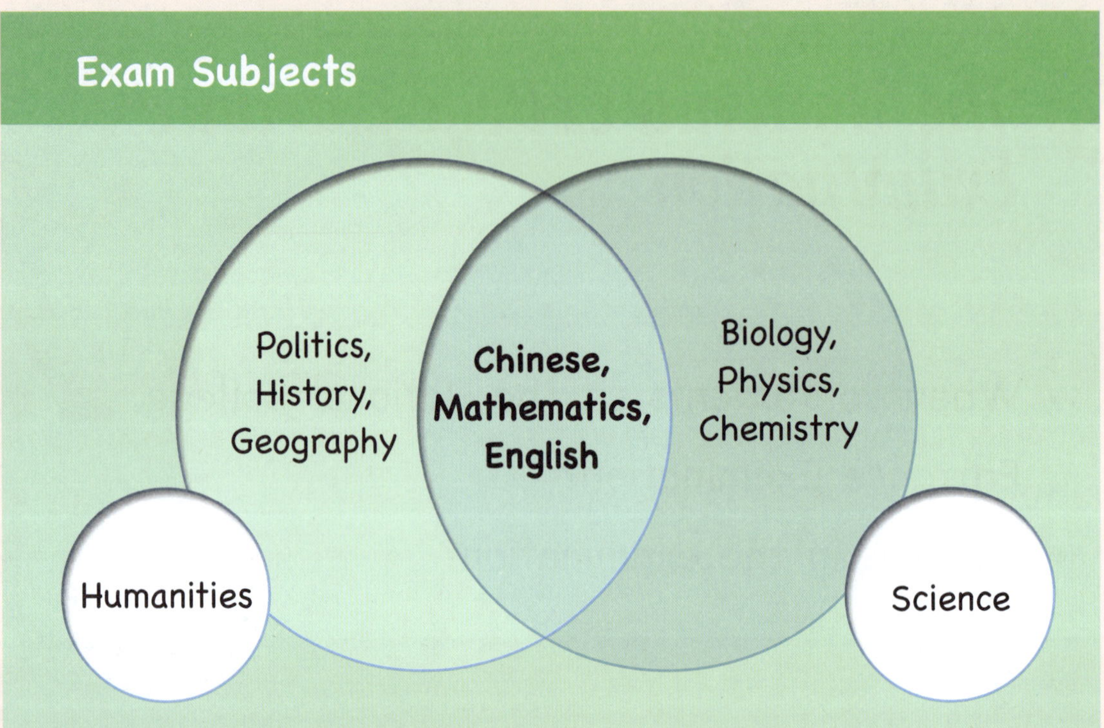

Do you know?
Students study for 12 years to prepare for this examination because it selects the top candidates for higher education.

More than 12 years of hard work

+

Competition with a large number of candidates

=

Entrance ticket to university

Tick the statements below that you think as true and EXPLAIN why you think so.

1. Confucius was an influential educator in Chinese history. .... □
2. Before the 15th century, girls could go to school. .... □
3. The first school similar to a Western school was set up in Beijing and called Jingshi Tongwenguan. .... □
4. The Confucian classics were based on the *Five Books* and the *Four Classics*. .... □
5. China was the first country in the world to introduce an official examination system. .... □
6. The Three-year Compulsory Education Law guarantees that all school-aged children receive at least three years of education. .... □
7. Primary school teachers tidy and clean the classrooms after school. .... □
8. Government officials are often chosen from the successful candidates of the National College Entrance Examination. .... □

Science and Technology

UNIT 6

1. The Four Great Inventions of Ancient China
2. Chinese Blue-and-white Porcelain
3. The Pioneers of Traditional Chinese Medicine
4. Zhang Heng and His Earthquake Detector
5. Yuan Longping: The Father of Hybrid Rice
6. Sending Humans into Space

Let's find out

- What are the Four Great Inventions of ancient China?
- What are China's major achievements in science and technology?

Let's watch a video

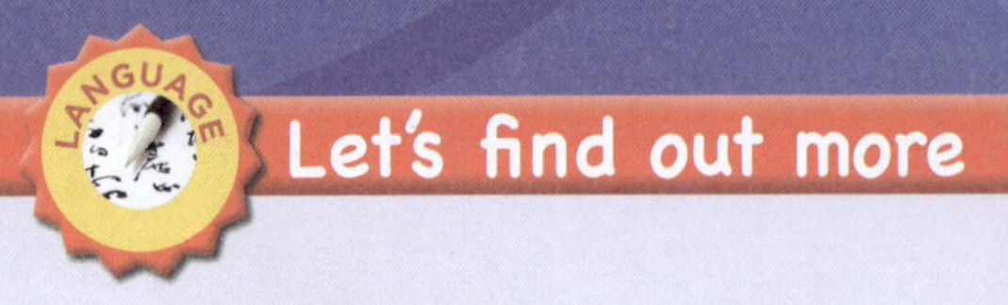

1. The Four Great Inventions of Ancient China

China is well-known for its Four Great Inventions which were made during the ancient times.

Paper-making

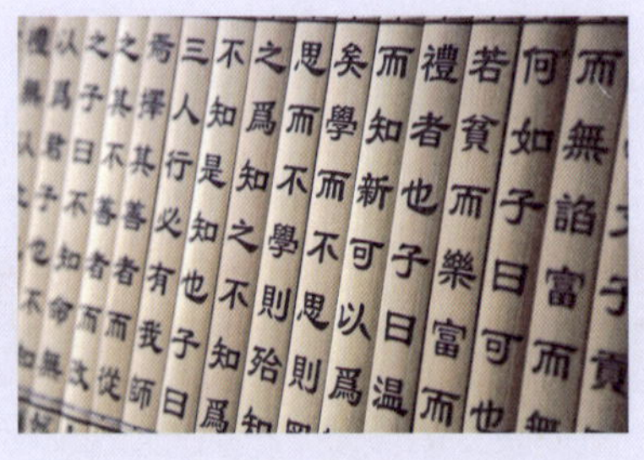

In ancient China, people used to write on pieces of bamboo and silk. During the Western Han Dynasty (206 BC–25 AD), people started using a rough type of paper which was made from plant fibres.

In the year 105, Cai Lun, a civil servant in the Eastern Han Dynasty (25-220), improved the technique of making paper by using mulberry bark, hemp rags, and old fishing nets as raw materials. Paper became cheaper, better looking and easier to write on.

By the 3rd century, paper had replaced the strips of bamboo and silk as the main

material used for writing, and the use of paper spread from China to the rest of the world in the 13th century.

Paper-making in Ancient China

1. Mix finely chopped bark and hemp rags with water and boil them.

2. Mash the boiled mixture flat, and then press out the water.

3. Dry the sheets in the sun.

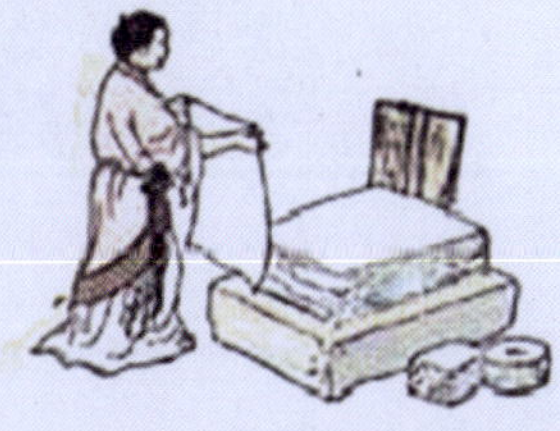

4. Check, peel and cut the dried paper.

The Compass

The compass may have been used during the 3rd century BC. During the Qin Dynasty (221 BC–206 BC), the world's first compass was created, which was called a "south-pointer" or "sinan". It was in the shape of a spoon, with its handle pointing to the south. The circular centre represented Heaven, and the square plate represented Earth.

The magnetic compass was used by sailors in ancient China during the 11th century. It was introduced to Europe 150 years later.

The plate was made from bronze.

The spoon-shaped compass was made from magnetic lodestone.

Printing

Before printing was invented, all writing was done by hand. This made books very expensive,

and only the richest people could afford them. During the Sui Dynasty (581-618), printing was invented. People carved words into wooden blocks, then inked the blocks and pressed paper on them to print a page.

This new technology developed during the 11th century. A man named Bi Sheng (990-1051) invented a new way of printing. He carved each Chinese character backwards on small blocks of fired clay. The blocks could be arranged to make sentences and texts. The same blocks could be reused to make many different texts. This method of printing was called "movable-type printing". This was a very important breakthrough in the technology of printing.

Gunpowder

Gunpowder was first discovered in China quite by accident by a group of religious people. In their quest for inventing "pills of immortality" (pills that would enable them to live forever), they found that a mixture of sulfur, saltpeter and charcoal could set off an explosion. They called the mixture "black powder".

This discovery led to the invention of fireworks, which began to be used in displays by emperors during the Tang Dynasty (around the year 700).

By the year 904, Chinese inventors had invented a variety of gunpowder weapons, such as flamethrowers, rockets, bombs, and land mines. They were used in wars.

The Chinese emperors tried to keep their discovery secret, but by the year 1100, their secret had leaked out. In the centuries that followed, the use of gunpowder spread from China, through the Middle East and then into Europe.

Activity time

1. Let's MAKE a cork and cup compass. You will need:
   - pins
   - a cork
   - water
   - a bar magnet
   - a clear plastic bowl or cup
   - a needle

2. Let's MAKE a sun compass. You will need:
   - a stick
   - a stone

   You need to try this invention on a sunny day, and outdoors.

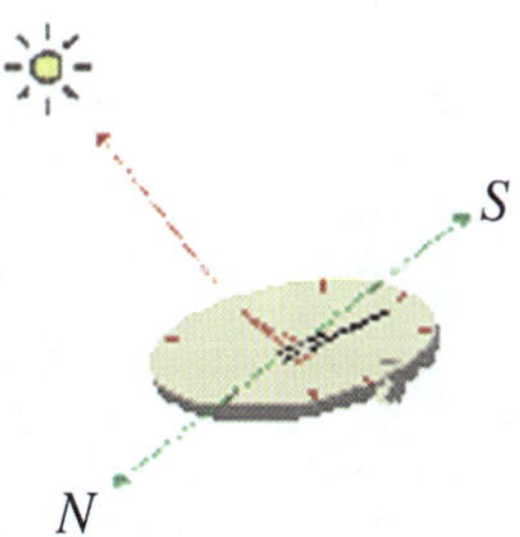

2. Chinese Blue-and-white Porcelain

- Why is porcelain also called "china"?
- What kind of porcelain is most famous?

Porcelain is often called "china" because China was the birthplace of porcelain making.

The very first objects made of porcelain appeared in China during the Shang Dynasty (1600 BC–1046 BC) and developed into the porcelain we know today during the Eastern Han Dynasty (25–220).

Porcelain making developed greatly during the Sui Dynasty (581–618) and the Tang Dynasty (618–907), and the most well-known objects were "tri-coloured glazed porcelain", called "Tangsancai" in Chinese.

Eventually, porcelain making spread to other areas of Asia and to Africa, and objects made of porcelain reached Europe during the Ming Dynasty (1368–1644).

The most famous type of Chinese porcelain in Europe were pieces that were finely painted blue-and-white in a style called "the ever-lasting blue flower".

Many places in China are famous for making porcelain products, and Jingdezhen is one of them. Known as the Capital of Porcelain, Jingdezhen is also one of the most famous cultural and historic cities in the country.

Activity time

DESIGN your own blue-and-white plate. The pattern below is one example.

3. The Pioneers of Traditional Chinese Medicine

- Who were the pioneers of traditional Chinese medicine?
- What did they achieve?

Hua Tuo

Three names are often mentioned in the history of traditional Chinese medicine: Hua Tuo, the founder of surgery; Zhang Zhongjing, the saint of Chinese medicine, and Li Shizhen, author of the first and most important Chinese medical book.

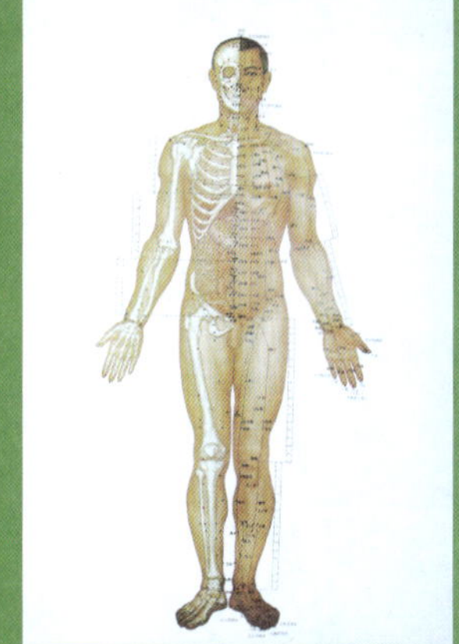

Hua Tuo (141–208) was a famous doctor who lived during the Eastern Han Dynasty (25–220).

He created a medicine called *mafeisan* which was made from herbs. He used the medicine during surgeries. It allowed patients to undergo surgeries without feeling pain. *Mafeisan* was the earliest known anaesthetic. It was not until over 1600 years later that countries in the West began to use general anaesthetics on patients during operations.

Hua Tuo was also an expert on needles. He used needles during a treatment called "acupuncture" which he performed on patients to relieve pain, treat disease and promote general health.

Hua Tuo also pioneered the idea of keeping fit to guard against illness. He invented the "Five-animal Exercises". These exercises involved imitating the movements of five animals: the tiger, the deer, the

The Five-animal Exercises

Tiger

Deer

Bear

Ape

Bird

Zhang Zhongjing

bear, the ape, and the bird. He believed that regular practice of these exercises would help keep people healthy.

Zhang Zhongjing, who also lived during the Eastern Han Dynasty (25–220), was another great man of medicine.

During the time, in the area where Zhang Zhongjing lived, there were frequent outbreaks of a terrible disease called typhoid. His despair at the loss of many of his family members to this terrible disease made Zhang decide to study medicine.

During his years of hard work, he wrote a 16-volume book called *Typhoid and Other Diseases*.

The book described ways of curing diseases and contained other important medical information. His pioneering work paved the way for future generations to study traditional Chinese medicine.

Li Shizhen was a famous medical specialist and chemist who lived during the Ming Dynasty (1368–1644). He was born into a family of doctors and became a doctor himself at the age of 24.

Li Shizhen was very interested in traditional Chinese medicine. He read many of the old medical books but

found that they contained many mistakes and were often confusing, so he became determined to write a better book.

He spent 30 years working on his book, during which time he collected thousands of herbs from different parts of the country.

He finished his book when he was 60 years old and he called it *Compendium of Materia Medica*. His book, with over 1000 pictures, contained information on over 1800 herbs that could be used as medicines and suggested over 10,000 cures for different illnesses. It was a ground-breaking medical book at the time and it is still used today.

The book has been translated into many languages and is often referred to as the "Great Chinese Medical Work".

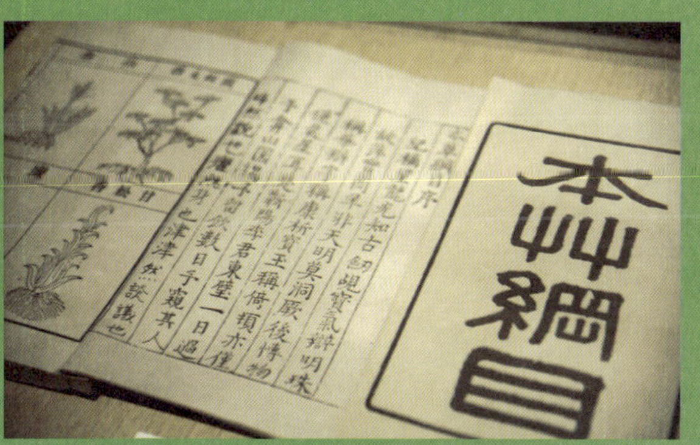

1. MATCH the person with his achievement.

Hua Tuo

Typhoid and Other Diseases

Zhang Zhongjing

Compendium of Materia Medica

Li Shizhen

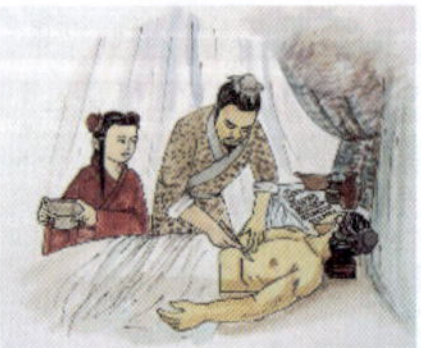
mafeisan

2. Let's LEARN to do the Five-animal Exercises.

4. Zhang Heng and His Earthquake Detector

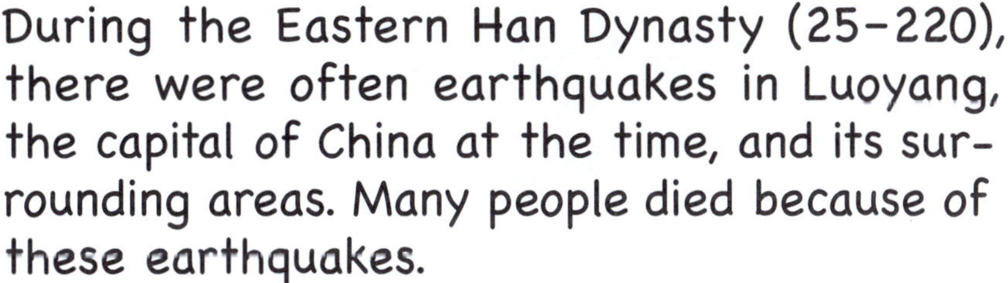

- Were there earthquakes in ancient China?
- How did scientists study earthquakes then?

During the Eastern Han Dynasty (25–220), there were often earthquakes in Luoyang, the capital of China at the time, and its surrounding areas. Many people died because of these earthquakes.

At the time, there lived a clever mathematician called Zhang Heng (78-139). He spent many years carefully studying these earthquakes and eventually invented an instrument that could pinpoint the exact direction of an earthquake from very far away.

The instrument was in the shape of a jar, and was made of copper and had eight bronze dragons attached to it, each facing a different direction. Under each dragon's head squatted a frog with an open mouth. Each dragon had a copper ball in its mouth which would fall into the mouth of the frog below if there was an earthquake in that direction.

In the year 133 and for the following four years,

Zhang Heng's instrument successfully pinpointed the location of earthquakes in the Luoyang area.

Zhang Heng's invention was the first of its kind in the world. It was not until the 13th century that similar instruments appeared outside China.

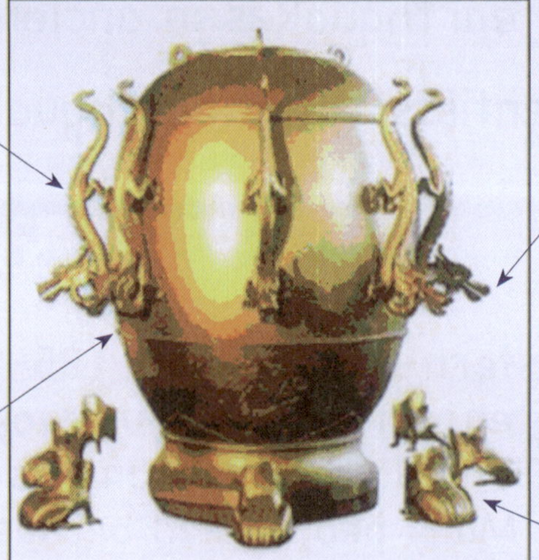

Let's listen to a story

Zhang Heng and His Earthquake Detector

Follow-up activities

1. Draw a picture of Zhang Heng's instrument.
2. Discussion:

- Why did Zhang Heng invent his earthquake detector?
- How did Zhang Heng's instrument work?
- Did Zhang Heng's instrument succeed in pinpointing the locations of all earthquakes?

Let's MAKE an earthquake detector. You will need:

- a cardboard box with the flaps cut off
- a plastic cup
- a marker
- a piece of string
- a cup of small rocks, marbles, or bolts
- clay
- paper
- scissors

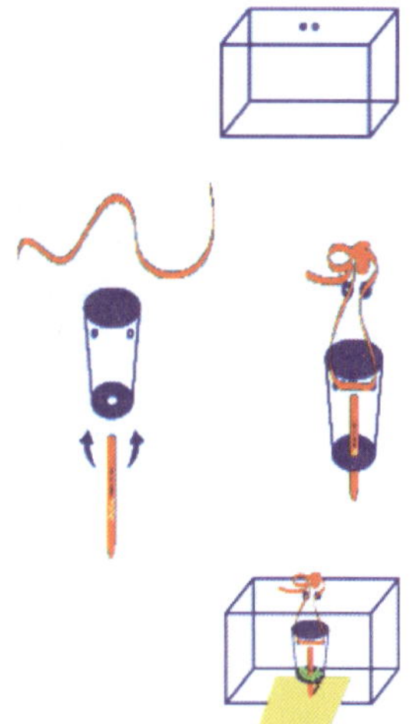

5. Yuan Longping: The Father of Hybrid Rice

- How important is rice to China, and to the world?
- What is "hybrid rice"? What is special about it?
- Who is Yuan Longping? What did he do?

During the 1970s, Chinese scientists succeeded in growing a very special breed of rice called "hybrid rice". The lead scientist involved with this project was Yuan Longping, well known throughout the world as the "father of hybrid rice". He used a new technique to grow a crop that could produce 30% more rice than ordinary breeds.

Yuan's hybrid rice has since been grown in many countries in Africa, America, and Asia. His discovery has allowed countries around the world to produce enough rice to feed more than 80 million people.

Over the recent decades, Yuan has developed another new "super hybrid rice". He believes that the development of these new types of crops is essential for combating famine.

Do you know?

Rice is a staple food for over 50% of the world's population. By 2030 the world will have to produce 60% more rice than it did in 1995 in order to feed its growing population.

LOOK at the pictures of food below and DECIDE which are made of rice. Can you NAME other foods that are made of rice?

Let's play a game
— Growing Rice

6. Sending Humans into Space

- How much do you know about space travels by mankind?
- Have any Chinese people been to space?

The first human flight into space was made by a Soviet astronaut on 12 April 1961.

China developed the ability to send humans into space a bit later, but in the early years of the 21st century, there were great developments in China's space programmes.

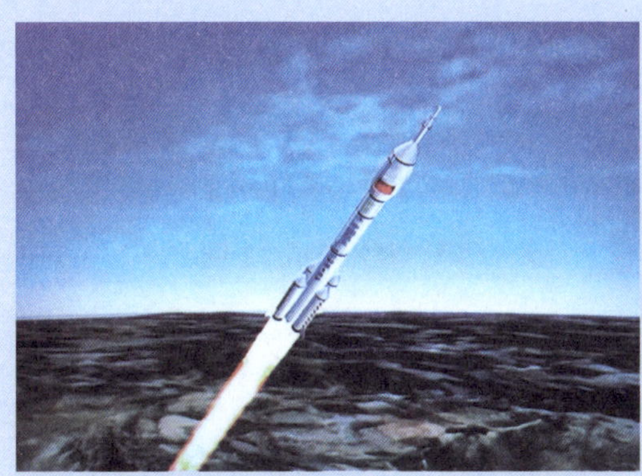

On 15 October 2003, a Chinese spacecraft, the Shenzhou-5, sent Yang Liwei, the first Chinese astronaut, into outer space. He orbited the earth 14 times before returning home safely.

Since then, China has become the third country, after Russia and the United States, to be able to send humans into space.

Since the launch of Shenzhou-5 in 2003, China has carried out five more space missions: Shenzhou-6 manned spaceship (12 October 2005), Shenzhou-7 manned spaceship (25 September 2008), Shenzhou-8 unmanned spaceship with two test dummies (31 October 2011) and Shenzhou-9 manned spaceship with a three-person crew including one female (16 June 2012). While in space, both Shenzhou-8 and Shenzhou-9 visited Tiangong-1, China's first unmanned space station launched on 29 September 2011.

The most recent space mission has been Shenzhou-10, launched on 11 June 2013. The spacecraft succeeded in docking with Tiangong-1, where an astronaut gave a 40-minute lecture on physics. The space lecture was telecast live across China with millions of school pupils watching it.

Do you know?
Spaceships are sent into outer space with the help of rockets.

Activity time

1. IMAGINE you are an astronaut and will be sent into outer space in a spaceship. What would you like to see in space? Why? IMAGINE what outer space looks like and draw a picture of it.

2. Let's MAKE a rocket. You will need:

- coloured paper
- an empty paper towel tube
- pencils, markers or crayons
- tape
- glue
- a ruler
- scissors

• coloured pens or stickers (optional)

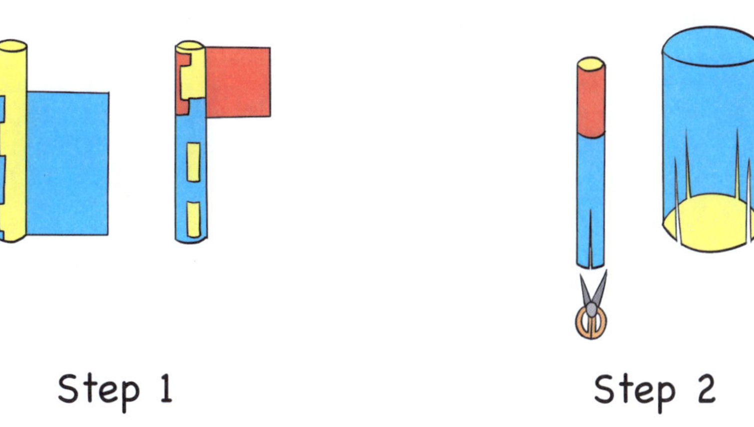

Step 1 Step 2

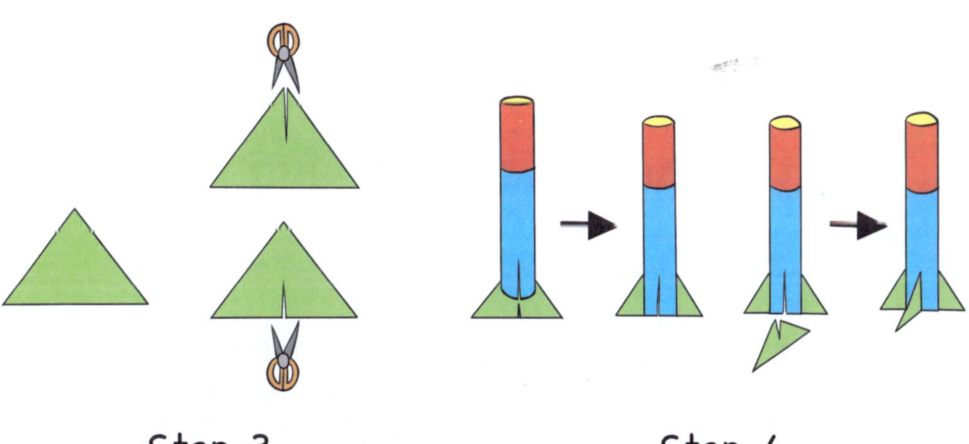

Step 3 Step 4

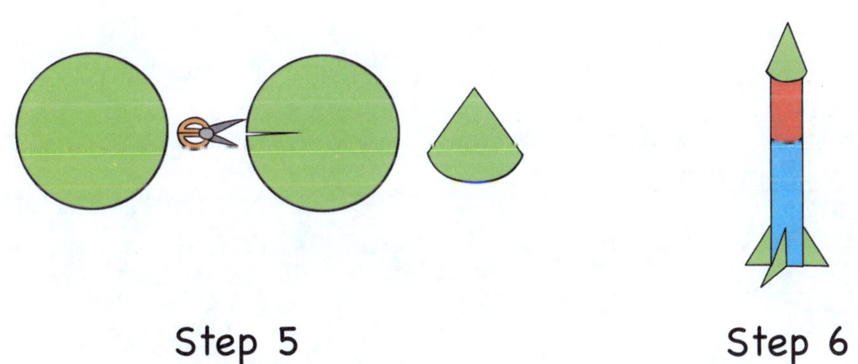

Step 5 Step 6

Festivals

UNIT 7

1. The Chinese Lunar Calendar
2. The Spring Festival
3. The Lantern Festival
4. The Tomb Sweeping Festival
5. The Dragon Boat Festival
6. The Mid-autumn Festival
7. China's National Day

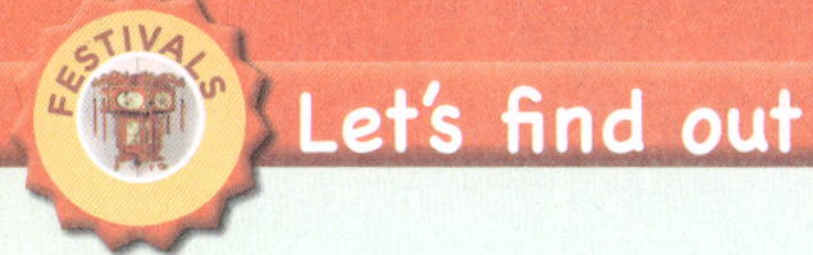

Let's find out

- What is the Chinese lunar calendar?
- What are the most popular traditional festivals in China?
- How do people celebrate these festivals?

Let's watch a video

1. The Chinese Lunar Calendar

The Chinese lunar calendar is based on the phases of the moon.

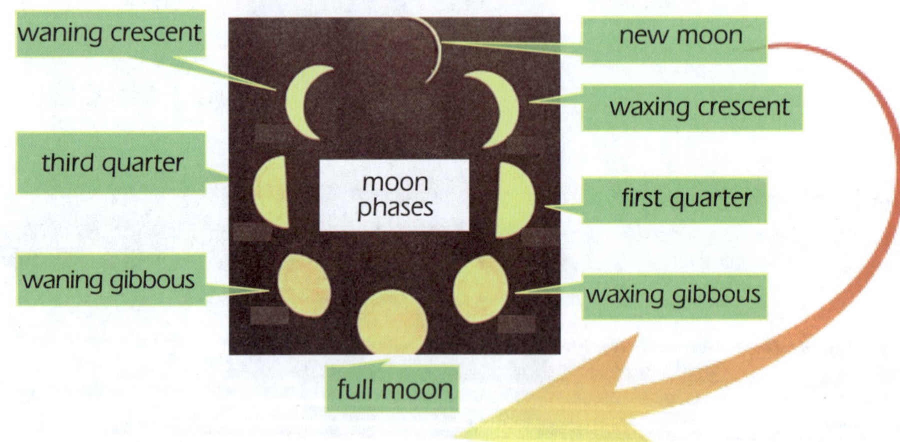

During a period of about 30 days, the moon goes through a complete set of phases: new, waxing crescent, first quarter, waxing gibbous, full, waning gibbous, third quarter, and waning crescent.

- There are 12 months in each calendar year.
- Each lunar month has either 29 or 30 days.
- Almost all Chinese festivals are based on the Chinese lunar calendar.

The Story of the 12 Animals

Follow-up activities

1. Write down the order of the animals in the Chinese zodiac.

2. Find out
   1. Which zodiac year is the coming year?
   2. In which zodiac year were you born?
   3. What are your family members' zodiac animals?

DRAW your Chinese zodiac animal and MAKE your own personality card.

2. The Spring Festival

- What is the Spring Festival?
- When is it?
- Why do Chinese people celebrate it and how do they celebrate?

The Spring Festival (also called the Chinese New Year) is the most important Chinese festival.

This is the time when family members gather together to celebrate, just like Christmas in the West.

The Spring Festival happens on the first day of the first month in the Chinese lunar calendar, usually in January or February in the Western calendar. The celebrations usually last for 15 days.

The most exciting days during the Chinese New Year are Spring Festival Eve and the following three days.

Activity time

LOOK at this 2015 calendar. Two dates have been circled: Spring Festival Eve (除夕) and the Spring Festival (春节).

2015年 2月

一	二	三	四	五	六	日
26 初七	27 腊八节	28 初九	29 初十	30 十一	31 十二	1 十三
2 十四	3 十五	4 十六	5 十七	6 十八	7 十九	8 二十
9 廿一	10 廿二	11 廿三	12 廿四	13 廿五	14 廿六	15 廿七
16 廿八	17 廿九	18 除夕	19 春节	20 初二	21 初三	22 初四
23 初五	24 初六	25 初七	26 初八	27 初九	28 初十	1 十一

FIND out when the Spring Festival falls in the coming year.

Let's Listen to a story

The Monster Nian

Follow-up activities

1. Why did people run away from their village on the New Year's Eve?

2. Did Nian eat the sick old man in the end? Why?

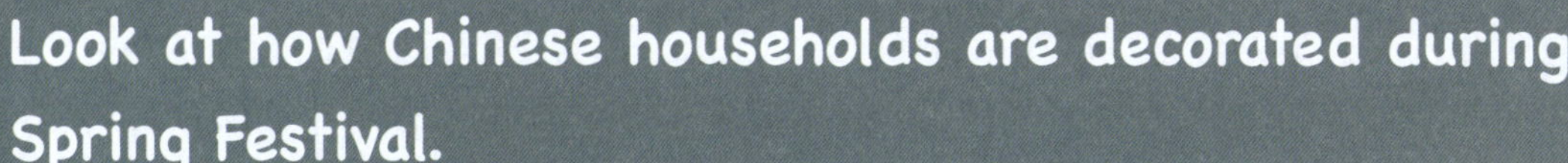

Look at how Chinese households are decorated during Spring Festival.

Character 福, a symbol of blessing, good fortune and good luck

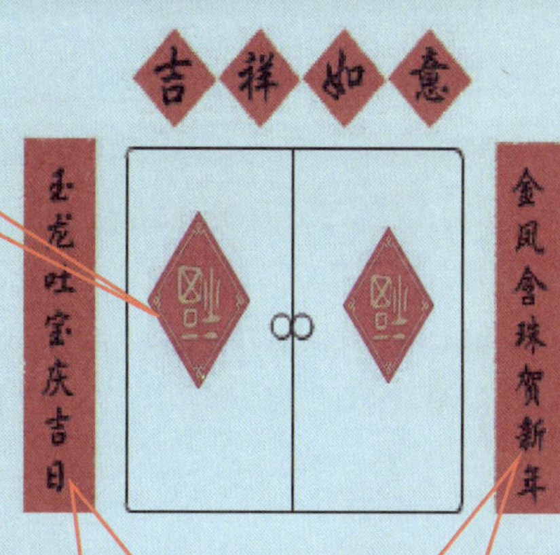

Antithetical couplet

Chinese New Year's poster

Paper cutting, usually pasted on windows

Look at what Chinese people eat on Chinese New Year's Eve.

Dumplings, in the shape of ancient gold bars, symbolising wealth.

A whole fish, pronounced as yú, with the same sound as "surpluses", symbolising togetherness and abundance.

A whole chicken (with head and feet), a symbol of completeness.

Look at what the children are most excited about at New Year's time.

Firecrackers and Red Envelopes

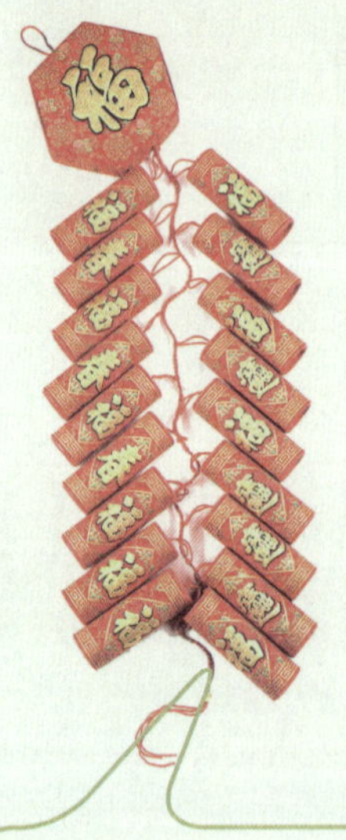

Setting off Firecrackers

This was originally intended to frighten away monsters. Now it has become a popular activity to celebrate the coming of a happy new year.

New Year Greetings

These four characters form a greeting, meaning "Congratulations and be prosperous!" It is a greeting commonly used during the Spring Festival.

Red Envelopes

Red is the colour used to ward off evil spirits, and the money inside is a symbol of fortune and wealth in the coming year.

The Lion Dance and the Dragon Dance

The Dragon Dance is performed for good weather and good harvests.

The Lion Dance wards off evil and brings good luck.

Watching the Chinese New Year Gala

After the Chinese New Year's Eve dinner, the whole family will often spend the night watching the New Year Gala on TV, which usually starts at around 8:00 pm and lasts until after midnight. People stay up for the night to welcome in the new year with great joy. This has become a tradition since 1983, when this special national TV programme was launched.

Spring Festival Decorations

Decorate the gate and room by dragging the items to their proper positions.

1. COLOUR the following images.

2. THINK of a festival you celebrate in your own country and COMPARE it with the Chinese Spring Festival.

	Spring Festival	Your festival
When is it?		
Why is it celebrated?		
How is it celebrated?		

Question: What do you like most about the Spring Festival?

3. MAKE a red envelope and WRITE lucky words in Chinese on your envelope.

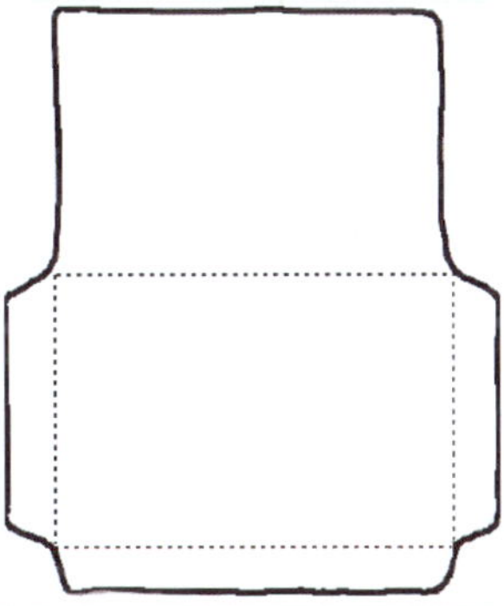

Jigsaw Puzzle

Drag and drop the scrambled pieces to make complete pictures. Guess what animals they are.

3. The Lantern Festival

- What is the Lantern Festival?
- When is it?
- How do Chinese people celebrate it?

The Lantern Festival falls on the 15th day of the 1st month in the Chinese lunar calendar, which is usually in February or March in the Western calendar. It also represents the end of the Spring Festival season.

2015年 ▾ ‹ 3月 ▾ › 假期安排 ▾ 返回今天

一	二	三	四	五	六	日
23 初五	24 初六	25 初七	26 初八	27 初九	28 初十	1 十一
2 十二	3 十三	4 十四	5 元宵节	6 十六	7 十七	8 十八
9 十九	10 二十	11 廿一	12 廿二	13 廿三	14 廿四	15 廿五
16 廿六	17 廿七	18 廿八	19 廿九	20 初一	21 初二	22 初三
23 初四	24 初五	25 初六	26 初七	27 初八	28 初九	29 初十
30 十一	31 十二	1 愚人节	2 十四	3 十五	4 十六	5 清明

The Lantern Festival is also called the "Yuanxiao Festival". During this festival people eat a special food called *yuanxiao*.

Find out when the Lantern Festival (元宵节) occurs this year.

Yuanxiao are balls made from sticky rice flour which are cooked and then served in boiling water. They can be small or large and contain fillings. They are also called "tangyuan", which sounds like "tuanyuan", meaning "reunion" in Chinese. People eat them hoping to bring reunion, harmony and happiness to the family.

Look at what people do during the Lantern Festival.

They enjoy eating *yuanxiao*.

They put up lanterns and watch lantern shows.

They solve lantern riddles.

COLOUR the lantern.

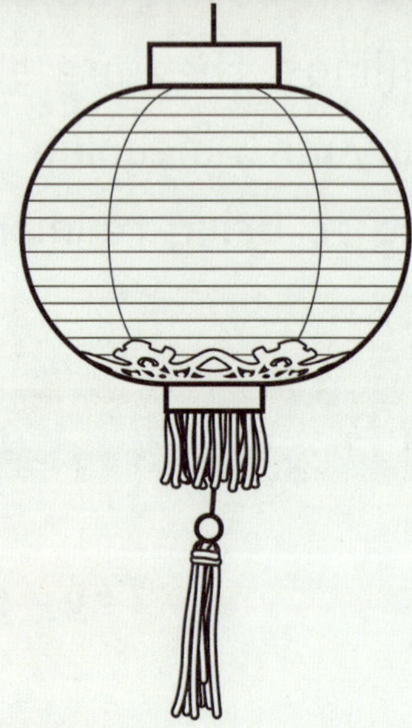

4. The Tomb Sweeping Festival

- What is the Tomb Sweeping Festival?
- When is it?
- Why do people observe it and what do they do?

The Tomb Sweeping Festival, also called the Qingming Festival, is the time when people visit the graves of their deceased family members and ancestors. It is also a celebration that marks an important season in the farming calendar.

The festival happens from the 4th to the 6th of April every year.

The Qingming Festival originated from Hanshi Day (literally, the Day of Cold Food), which was a memorial day for Jie Zitui, who died in 636 BC during the Spring and Autumn Period.

Jie Zitui was one of the many followers of Duke Wen of the State of Jin.

Duke Wen was exiled for 19 years. He and his followers often suffered from hunger. One day, Jie cut a piece of meat from his own thigh to make some soup for Wen. Wen was so moved that he promised to reward Jie some day.

However, many years went by, Duke Wen forgot to reward Jie, who by then had moved into the forest with his mother. Eventually, Duke Wen went to the forest, but could not find Jie. He ordered his men to set fire to the forest to force Jie out.

Unfortunately, Jie died in the fire. Filled with remorse, Duke Wen ordered that no fire be used to cook food for three days in memory of Jie.

Since then, it has become a tradition for people to visit the graves of their deceased family members and ancestors during the Qingming season. They sweep the graves, offer sacrifices, burn incenses and "spirit money", and set off firecrackers. Nowadays, however, changes have taken place and "spirit money" and firecrackers are replaced by flowers.

Many people also fly kites during the Qingming Festival.

1. LOOK at the picture showing what people do when they visit their ancestors' tombs during the Qingming Festival. Can you WRITE down a short phrase in each space provided below, telling what they are doing?

____

____

____

____

2. Can you DRAW a kite like this? MAKE your kite as colourful as possible.

5. The Dragon Boat Festival

- When is the Dragon Boat Festival?
- Why do people celebrate it?
- How do people celebrate it?

The Dragon Boat Festival happens on the 5th day of the 5th month in the Chinese lunar calendar, usually in May or June in the Western calendar.

The Dragon Boat Festival is in memory of Qu Yuan (340 BC-278 BC), a very well-known poet who was very patriotic,

but unfortunately the king he served did not take his advice.

When the State of Qin conquered Qu Yuan's state, he lost all hope and drowned himself in a river on the 5th day of the 5th month of the Chinese lunar

calendar in 278 BC.

People loved Qu Yuan and wanted to save his body from being eaten by the fish, so they threw *zongzi* (sticky rice dumplings wrapped in bamboo leaves) into the river for the fish to eat instead.

They also sent out boats to recover his body. From then on, boat-racing and eating *zongzi* have become a national tradition.

Look at what people do during the Dragon Boat Festival.

They watch dragon boat racing.

They enjoy eating *zongzi*.

Zongzi are made of sticky rice stuffed with different fillings and wrapped in bamboo or reed leaves. They are cooked by steaming or boiling.

1. Dragon Boat Racing

Compete against the computer in the race by beating the drums.

2. Saving Qu Yuan's Body

Save Qu Yuan by throwing food into the water to feed the fish.

6. The Mid-autumn Festival

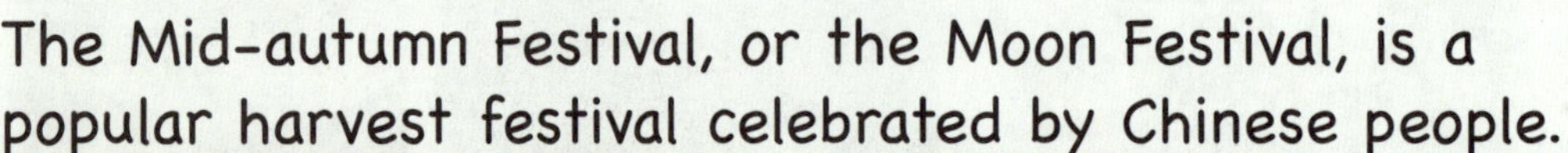

- What is the Mid-autumn Festival?
- When is it?
- Why do people celebrate it and what do they do?

The Mid-autumn Festival, or the Moon Festival, is a popular harvest festival celebrated by Chinese people.

It happens on the 15th day of the 8th month in the Chinese lunar calendar, usually in September or October in the Western calendar.

Here is a popular tale about the origin of the Moon Festival.

Legend has it that in ancient times there were ten suns in the sky. It was very hot and people were dying from extreme heat. Crops and plants could hardly survive.

To save people, a hero and archer named Hou Yi shot down nine of the ten suns. As a reward, the Queen of Heaven gave him a magic pill that would make him live forever. Once he took it he would become a god in Heaven. Hou Yi had a beautiful wife Chang'e. They lived happily on the earth and he would not even think of parting with her. He gave the pill to his wife, asking her to keep it for him.

One day, while Hou Yi went hunting, a man sneaked into his home, trying to seize the pill. He forced Chang'e to give it to him. In desperation, Chang'e quickly put the pill in her mouth and swallowed it. Then, something amazing happened. She started to float in the air, getting higher and higher in the sky, and finally, landed on the moon.

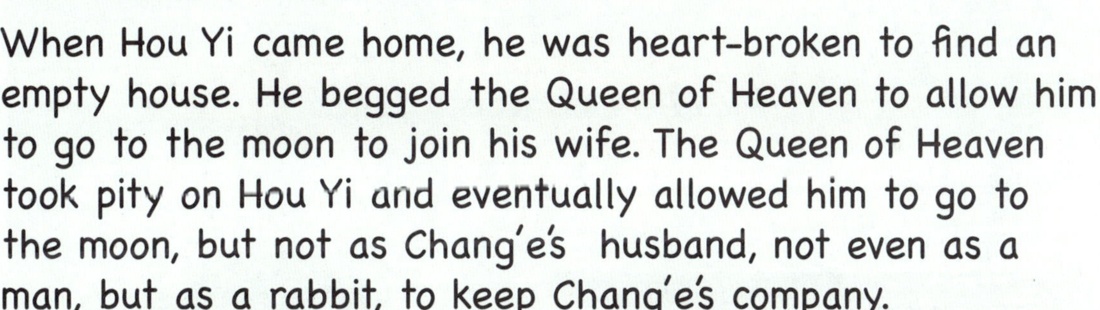

When Hou Yi came home, he was heart-broken to find an empty house. He begged the Queen of Heaven to allow him to go to the moon to join his wife. The Queen of Heaven took pity on Hou Yi and eventually allowed him to go to the moon, but not as Chang'e's husband, not even as a man, but as a rabbit, to keep Chang'e's company.

So, you see, everywhere Chang'e goes, she has a little rabbit with her. We don't know whether Chang'e had any idea of who the lovely white rabbit is!

The Moon Festival has since become an occasion when people celebrate family reunion and express warm feelings for their beloved. They enjoy drinking tea together and eating moon cakes.

People enjoy the full moon.

The moon is at its fullest and roundest on that day.

It is regarded as a perfect moment when someone catches the moon's reflection in the centre of his or her teacup.

People eat moon cakes.

Typical moon cakes are round, with a thick filling, usually made from lotus seed paste, and surrounded by a thin crust. Some moon cakes may contain the yolk of duck eggs.

COLOUR the image of Chang'e.

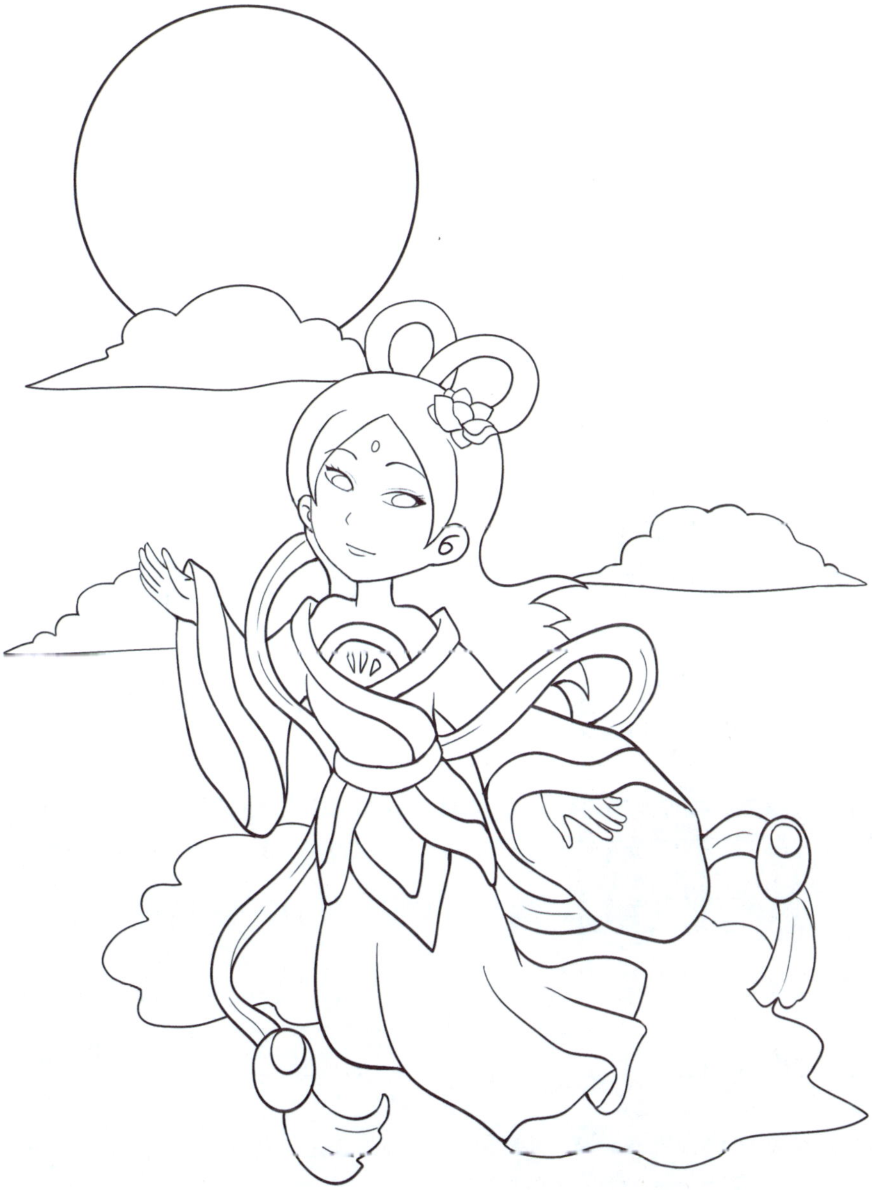

7. China's National Day

The National Day of China is celebrated every year on the 1st of October. It is a 3-day public holiday, but together with the two weekends at the beginning and the end of the holiday, people can have a whole week off. They enjoy this "Golden Week" very much.

The National Day is celebrated throughout China. The government organises a variety of activities, including firework displays and concerts. Public places, such as Tian'anmen Square in Beijing, are all decorated with lanterns and colourful hangings.

MAKE lanterns to DECORATE your classroom.

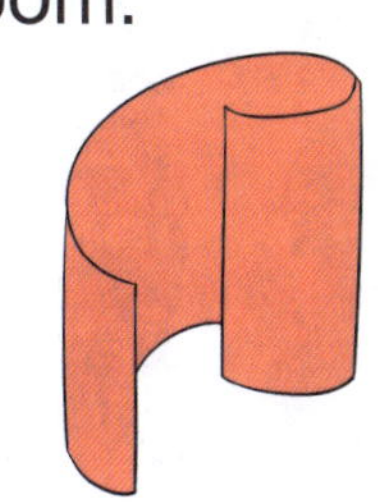

Step 1: Fold a rectangular piece of paper in half to form a long thin rectangle.

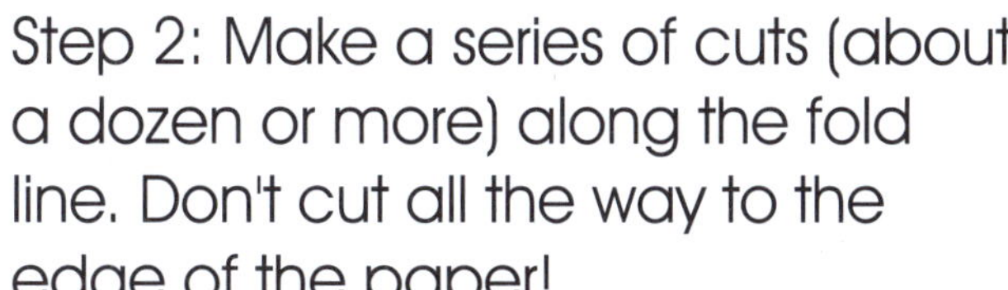

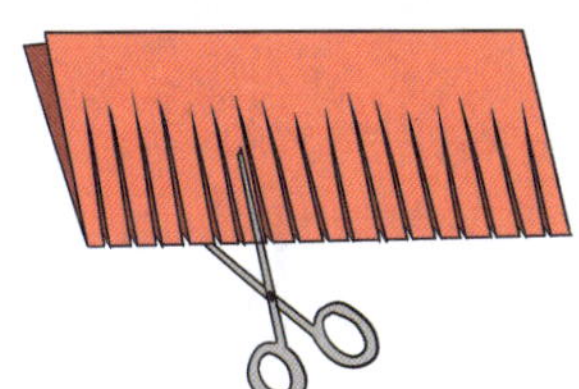

Step 2: Make a series of cuts (about a dozen or more) along the fold line. Don't cut all the way to the edge of the paper!

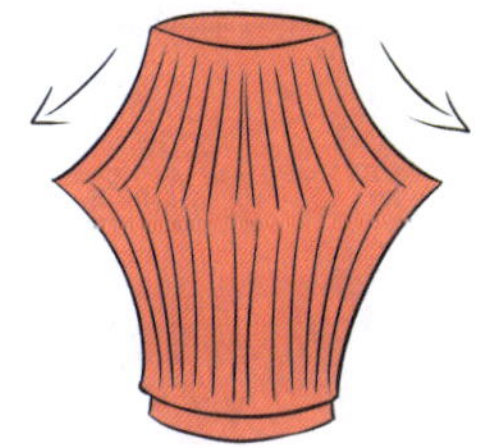

Step 3: Unfold the paper. Glue or staple the short edges of the paper together.

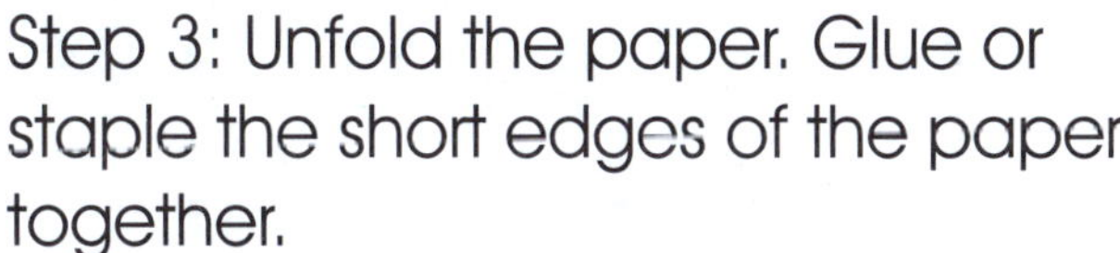

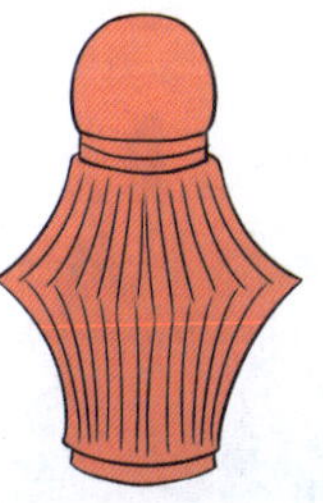

Step 4: Cut a strip of paper: six inches long and half an inch wide. Glue or staple this strip of paper to the lantern to make a lantern handle.

Make as many lanterns as you want in different colours. Then, hang them up to decorate your classroom.

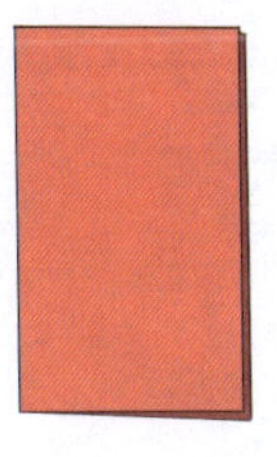

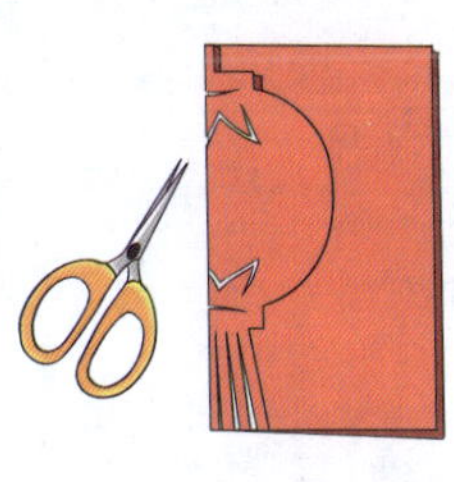

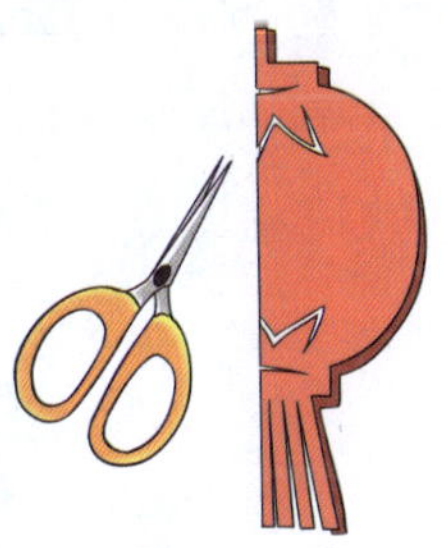

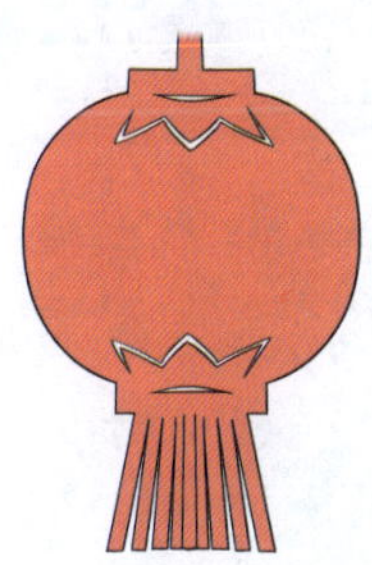

Tourism

UNIT 8

1. The Great Wall
2. The Forbidden City
3. Other Tourist Attractions in Beijing
4. The Terracotta Army
5. Huangshan Mountain
6. Other Well-known Mountains in China

Let's find out

- What are the most popular tourist attractions in China?
- Why are these sites famous?

Let's watch a video

1. The Great Wall

- Where is the Great Wall?
- When and why was the Great Wall built?
- What makes the Great Wall special?

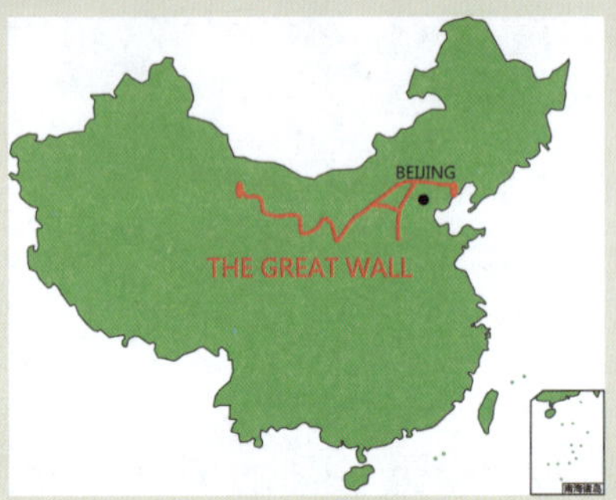

The Great Wall is in northeastern China. It stretches over 6700 km (4163 miles) along the country from east to west.

The Great Wall is over 2000 years old and dates back to ancient China, when Qin Shi Huang of the Qin Dynasty, the first emperor of China, ordered his people to build a huge wall to keep his enemies out of his lands.

He spent over 20 years on the project, forcing over two million people to build the Great Wall.

Since the time of Qin Shi Huang, the Great Wall has been repaired, rebuilt and expanded over the course of many dynasties, particularly during the Ming Dynasty (1368-1644). It was during this time that the main part of the Great Wall was

built and made into what we see today.
The Great Wall is made up of hundreds of passes or gates, fortresses and towers. The three best-known passes are the Jiayu Pass, the Juyong Pass and the Shanhai Pass.

Jiayu Pass

Juyong Pass

Shanhai Pass

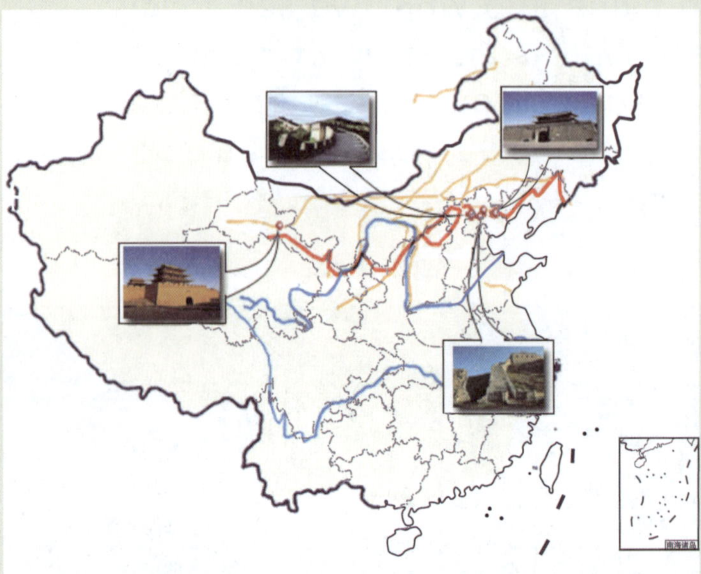

The four main tourist attractions along the Great Wall are the four sections called Badaling, Mutianyu, Jinshanling and Simatai.

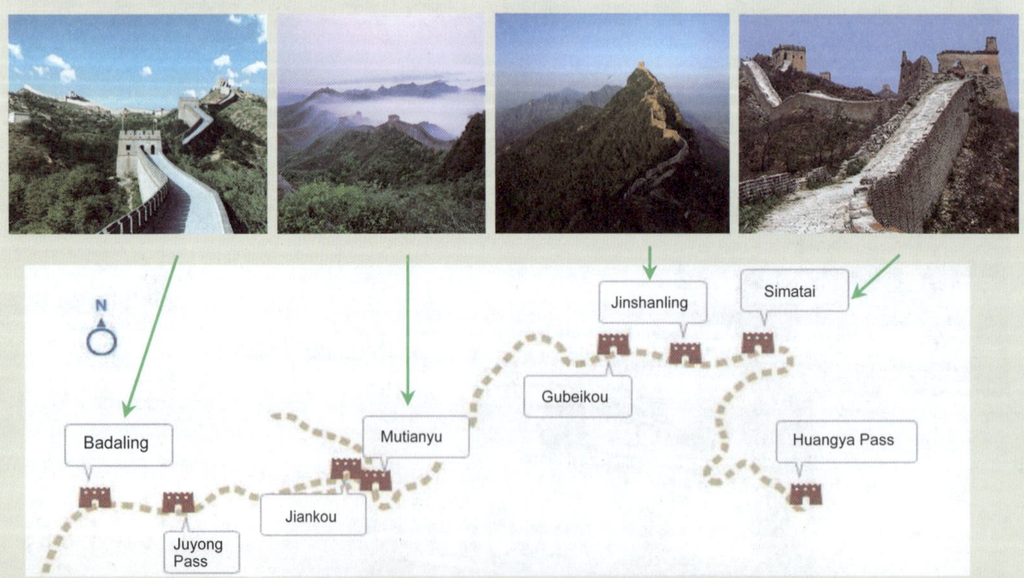

Among these four sites, Badaling in Beijing is the most famous. The path of the wall in Badaling is on average 7.8 metres high and 5.8 metres wide.

On top of Badaling is a famous monument with an inscription from Chairman Mao. It says: "He who has never been to the Great Wall is not a true man."

Over the years, many foreign celebrities and heads of state have visited the Great Wall, including the U.S. President Barack Obama and British Prime Minister David Cameron.

The Great Wall is one of the Seven Wonders of the World, and was listed by UNESCO (United Nations Educational, Scientific and Cultural Organisation) as a World Cultural Heritage Site in 1987.

Look how beautiful the Great Wall is in different seasons!

Spring

Summer

Autumn

Winter

Travel Tip

Don't leave your visit to the Great Wall to the last day of your trip to China because you will need a lot of energy for going up the mountains.

DRAW your own picture of the Great Wall. USE the following one as an example.

The Great Wall Jigsaw Puzzle

Drag and drop the scrambled pieces to make a complete picture of the Great Wall.

2. The Forbidden City

- Where is the Forbidden City?
- When was it built?
- What is special about it?

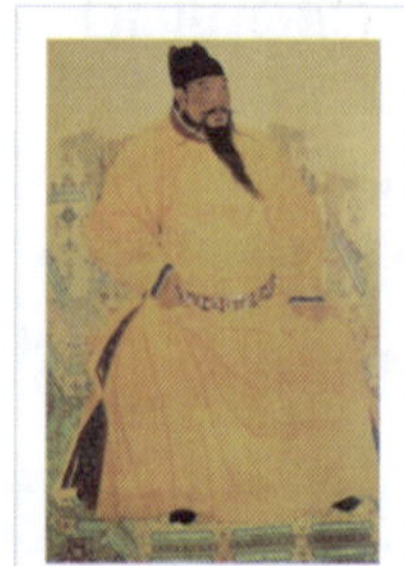

Tourism

The Forbidden City is in the very heart of Beijing.

The Forbidden City was a grand palace built by Emperor Yongle of the Ming Dynasty (1368-1644) when Beijing became capital of the country.

The building started in 1406 and was completed in 1420. Since then, it has been home to 24 emperors of the Ming and Qing dynasties.

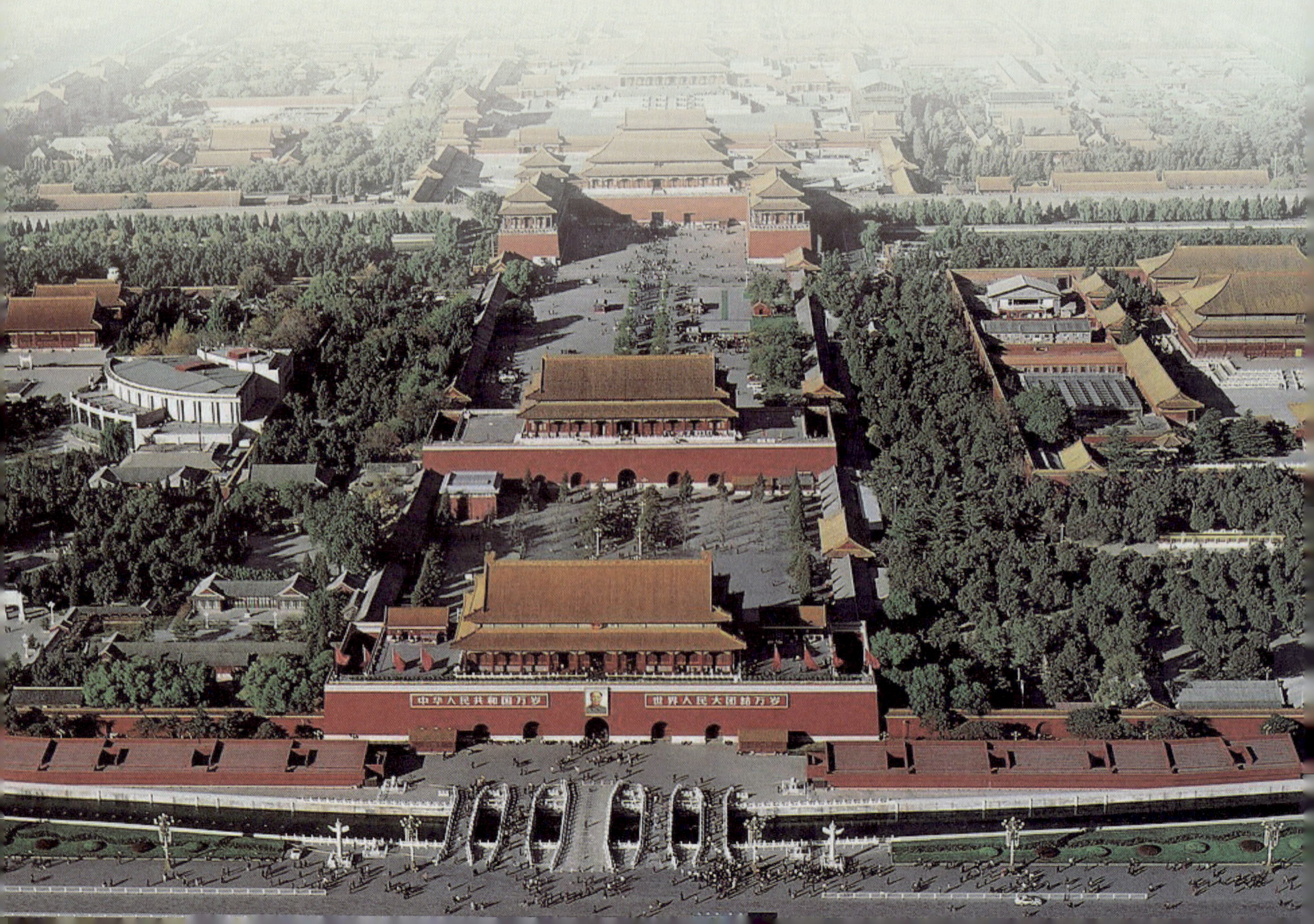

The Forbidden City covers an area of 720,000 square metres, consisting of 980 buildings and 8704 rooms. The palace is divided into two parts: the Outer (Front) Court and the Inner (Back) Court.

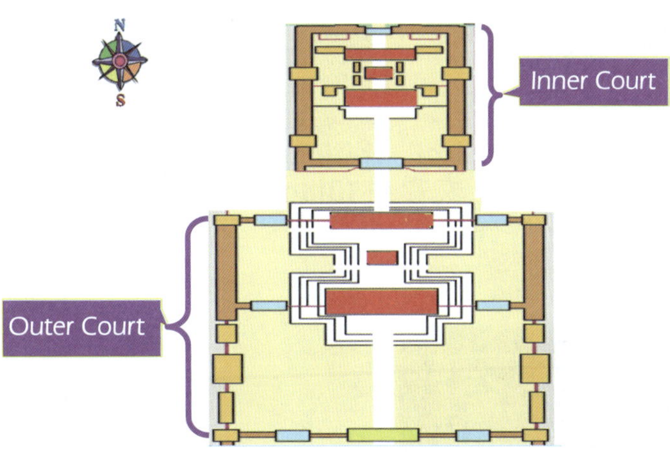

There are three halls in the Outer Court:

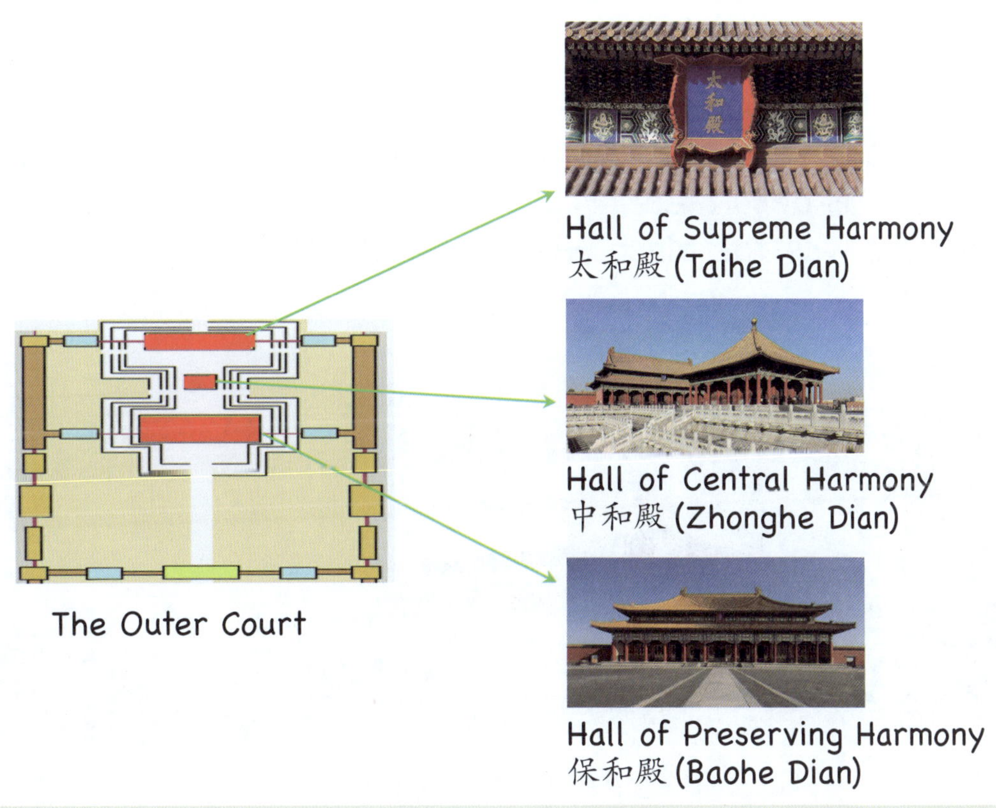

The Outer Court

Hall of Supreme Harmony
太和殿 (Taihe Dian)

Hall of Central Harmony
中和殿 (Zhonghe Dian)

Hall of Preserving Harmony
保和殿 (Baohe Dian)

There are also three halls in the Inner Court:

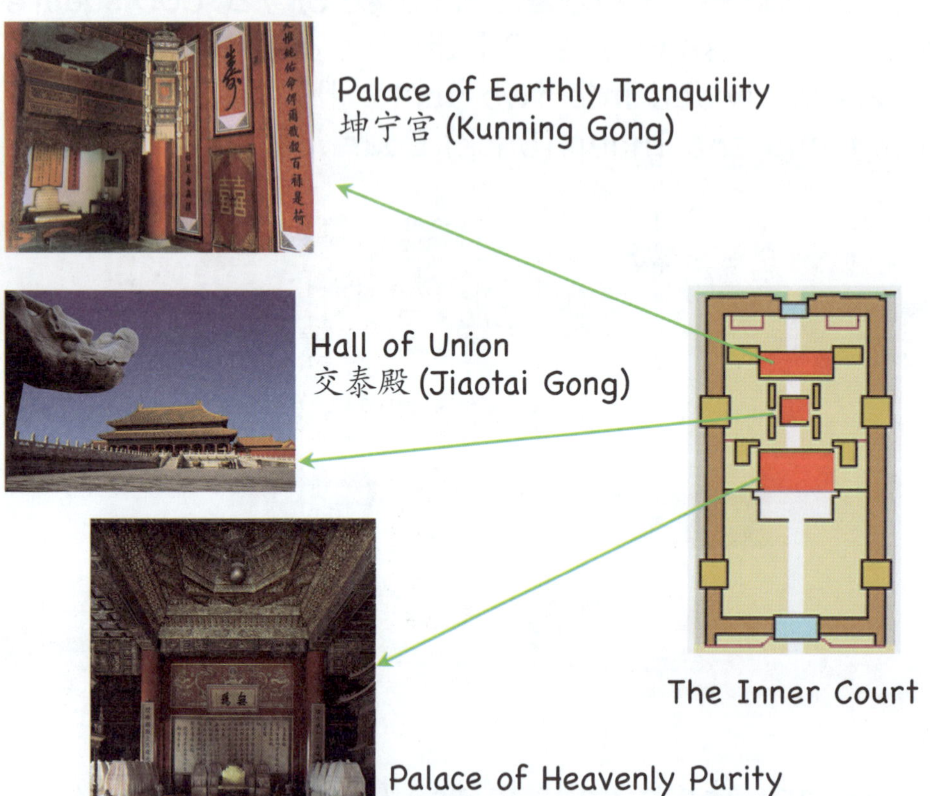

Among the six halls, the Hall of Supreme Harmony is the most important. It is decorated in red and gold and carved with dragons. This was the place where the emperors held grand ceremonies.

Hall of Supreme Harmony

Inside of the Hall

Emperor Throne

Within the halls, there are galleries full of precious works of art.

The Forbidden City is enclosed by walls that are over ten metres high. In ancient times, it was a place that ordinary people were forbidden to enter. Surrounding the Forbidden City and outside the walls there is a moat which is 52 metres wide.

Question
Can you guess why the moat was built?

Standing in each corner of the Forbidden City is a magnificent watch tower, which used to be heavily guarded.

There are many stone lions guarding the Forbidden City.

Do you know?
The male lion has a ball under his paw, and the female lion has a cub under her paw.

The Forbidden City is the largest palace made of wood in the world. It was declared a World Heritage Site in 1987.

Now the Forbidden City is a public museum and one of the most popular tourist attractions in China.

Travel Tip

Allow at least three hours for a brief tour of the Forbidden City and a whole day for an intensive tour. There are no restaurants inside the Forbidden City, though you can buy snacks and drinks there.

The Story of the 9999 and a Half Rooms

Follow-up activities

1. What was Emperor Yongle's dream?
2. Why was Emperor Yongle frightened and worried after he woke up?
3. How many rooms were built in Emperor Yongle's grand palace?
4. Imagine a conversation between Emperor Yongle and his clever adviser, Liu Bowen. Perform your role play.

Touring the Imperial Palace

Click the sites to know more about the Imperial Palace.

3. Other Tourist Attractions in Beijing

Apart from the Great Wall and the Forbidden City, there are other scenic spots you can visit in Beijing, notably the Summer Palace and the Temple of Heaven.

The Summer Palace

The Summer Palace is the largest and most well preserved imperial garden in China.

The Summer Palace has a 17-Arch Bridge, which is 150 metres long and has 544 stone lions on its railings.

Within the Summer Palace there is also the Long Corridor, which is over 700 metres long with paintings on all the beams.

The Temple of Heaven

The Temple of Heaven was where the emperors of the Ming and Qing dynasties prayed to Heaven for its blessings.

Some of the best-known scenic spots in the Temple of Heaven include:

The Hall of Prayer for Good Harvests

The Imperial Vault of Heaven

The Circular Mound Altar

The Echo Wall

4. The Terracotta Warriors

- How were the Terracotta Warriors discovered?
- What is special about them?

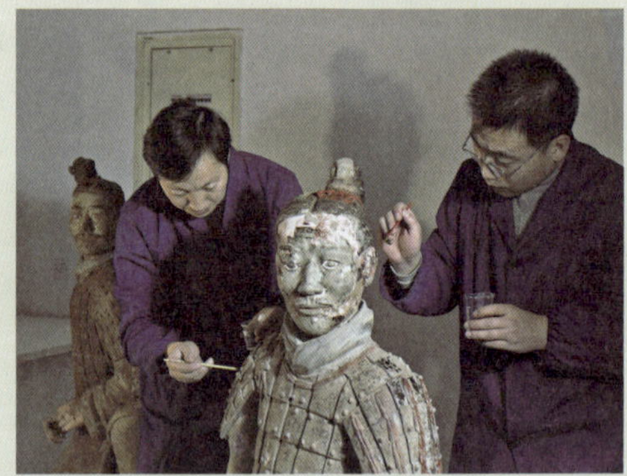

The Terracotta Warriors were discovered in 1974 by some local farmers in the eastern suburb of Xi'an in central China, whilst they were digging a well.

They found the relics of terracotta sculptures of ancient soldiers, horses and chariots buried under the ground.

Pit No. 1

Pit No. 2

According to archaeologists, this is the Terracotta Army that was buried with the first Emperor Qin Shi Huang over 2000 years ago.

Since 1974, archaeologists have further discovered three pits with terracotta warriors, horses and chariots together with weapons.

In Pit No. 1 there are over 6000 figures, standing in formation as if on a battlefield. They have been allowed to be seen by the public since 1979.

Pit No. 2 is L-shaped. It is the most spectacular of the three pits. The soldiers stand in battle lines and look as if they were of an important rank.

Pit No. 3

Pit No. 3 looks as if it was the headquarters of the army. There are 68 terracotta figures, four horses and a wooden chariot in this pit.

It is estimated that there are 8000 soldiers, 130 chariots with 520 horses, and 150 cavalry horses. The majority of them are still buried.

The Terracotta Warriors are life sized figures made of fired pottery, and each soldier's face looks different.

The Pottery Horses

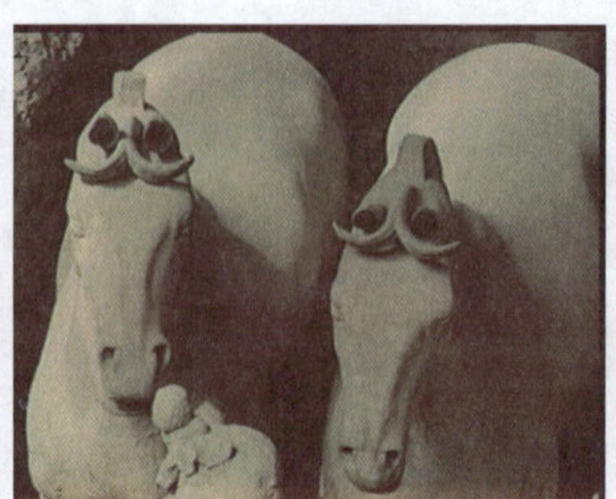

All the Terracotta Warriors were broken when they were found but have since been repaired.

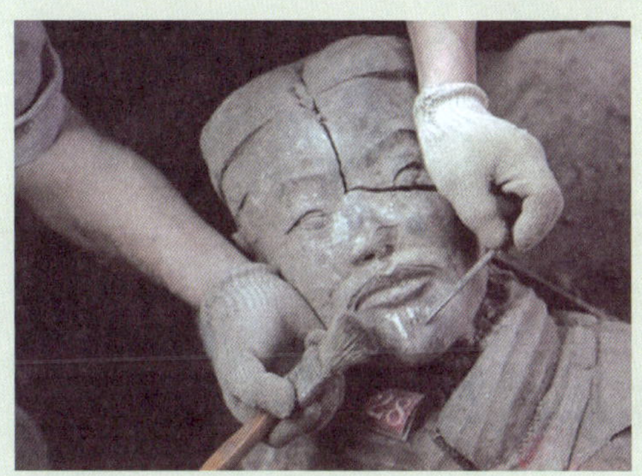

Activity time

1. Make a sketch of a Terracotta Warrior.

2. Draw your own picture of the terracotta warriors. Use the following as an example.

Terracotta Figure Jigsaw Puzzle

Join the pieces together to discover the terracotta figure.

5. Huangshan Mountain

- Where is it?
- Why is it so famous?

Huangshan Mountain is in southern Anhui Province in eastern China.

Huangshan Mountain is known for its three peaks: the Lotus Peak (1864m high), the Bright Summit Peak (1840m high), and the Celestial Peak (1829m high).

Lotus Peak

Bright Summit Peak

Celestial Peak

Huangshan is also famous for its four natural scenes: the unique rock formations, the waterfalls, the pine trees growing out of the rocks, and the sea of clouds surrounding the mountains. Huangshan Mountain has been listed as a UNESCO World Cultural and Natural Heritage Site.

Sunrise in Huangshan Mountain

The Monkey Watching the Sea

The Nine Dragons Waterfall

Sea of Clouds

Ying Ke Pine
(Welcoming Guests Pine)

Travel Tip
November to May is the best season for cloud viewing on Huangshan Mountain.

6. Other Well-known Mountains in China

Apart from Huangshan, there are other five mountains that are very famous in China. They are Mt. Taishan, Mt. Huashan, Mt. Hengshan, Mt. Songshan and Mt. Hengshan. Each has its own unique scenery.

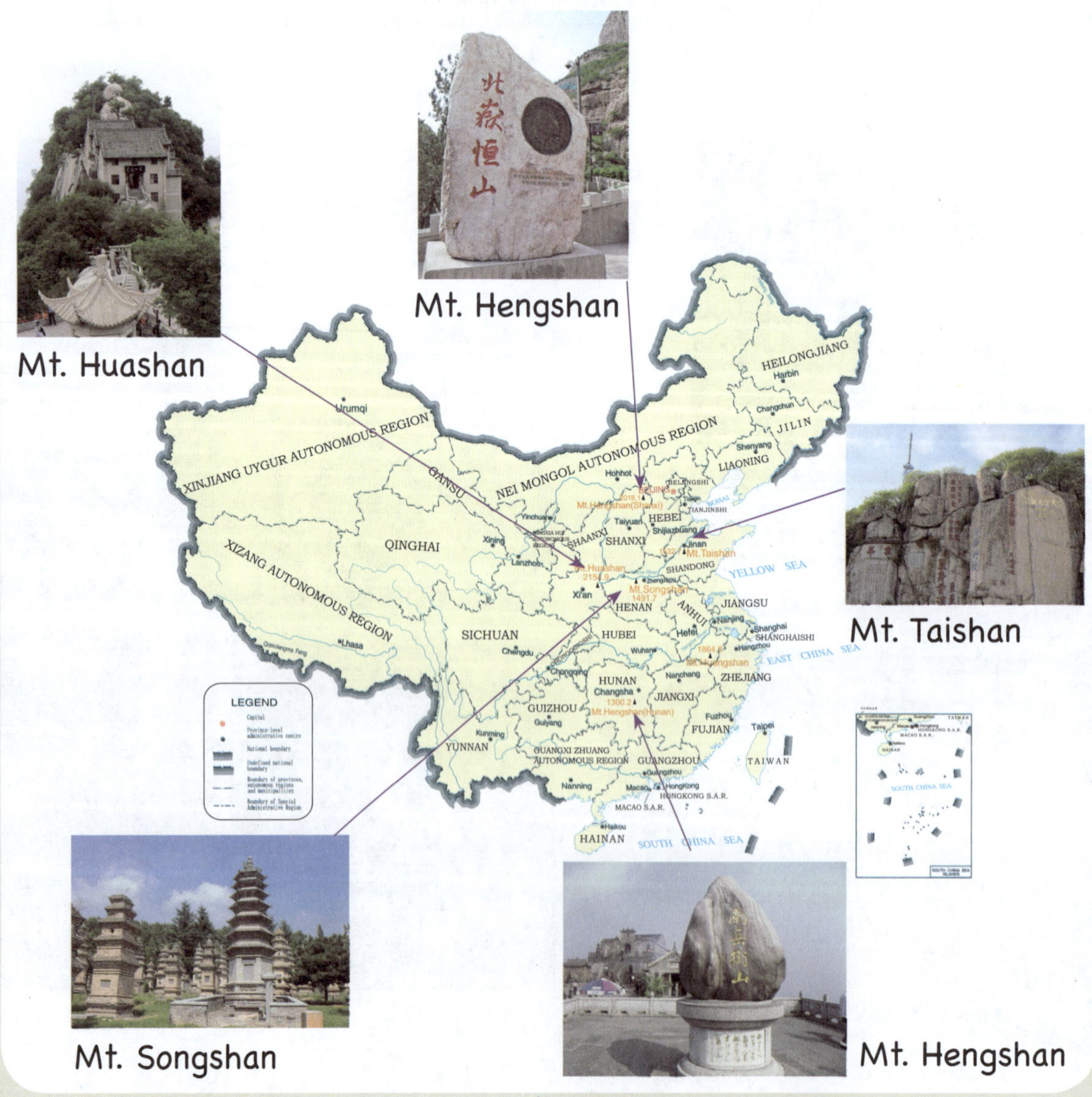

Mt. Huashan

Mt. Hengshan

Mt. Taishan

Mt. Songshan

Mt. Hengshan

The well-known Shaolin Temple is located on Mt. Songshan.

It is said to be the "No. 1 Temple under Heaven", where Shaolin monks practise *qigong*, or breathing exercises, and Shaolin *kungfu* (martial arts).

1. WRITE the Chinese character **山**.

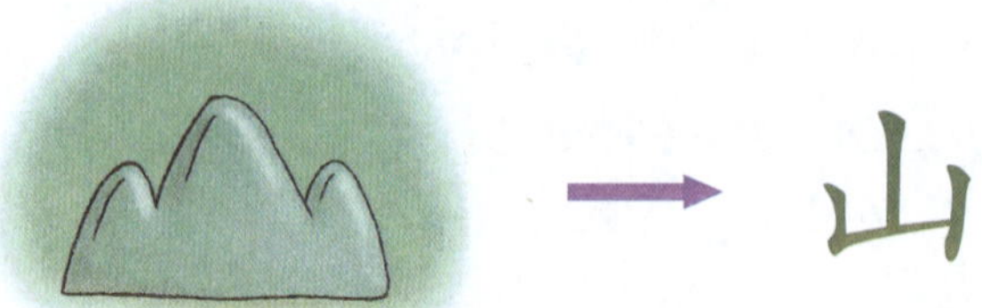

2. CREATE your own Chinese painting.

3. IMAGINE you are going to China for a week. PLAN your trip. COMPARE it with a friend's and EXPLAIN why you have chosen the places to visit.

Plan / Days	Places to visit	Things to see or do
Day 1		
Day 2		
Day 3		
Day 4		
Day 5		
Day 6		
Day 7		

责任编辑：翟淑蓉
英文编辑：薛彧威
封面设计：Daniel Gutierrez

图书在版编目（CIP）数据

发现中国：中国文化小学生读本. / 傅似逸著. —北京：华语教学出版社, 2015
ISBN 978-7-5138-0639-8

Ⅰ. ①发… Ⅱ. ①傅… Ⅲ. ①汉语－对外汉语教学－语言读物②中华文化－基本知识－汉、英 Ⅳ. ①H195.5②K203

中国版本图书馆CIP数据核字 (2014) 第054321号

地图审图号：GS (2014) 1896号

发现中国

主编 傅似逸
编者 胡爱琳 杨泛芝 彭丽 严蔚琳
英文编审 Nia Jones
*

华语教学出版社有限责任公司出版
（中国北京百万庄大街24号 邮政编码100037）
电话: (86)10-68320585, 68997826
传真: (86)10-68997826, 68326333
网址：www.sinolingua.com.cn
电子信箱：hyjx@sinolingua.com.cn
新浪微博地址：http://weibo.com/sinolinguavip
北京诚顺达印刷有限公司印刷
2015年（16开）第1版
ISBN 978-7-5138-0639-8
定价：99.00元